Come For Fun

Sexy Stories Collection

VOLUME 9

16 EROTIC SHORT STORIES

MELISA POCHE

Publisher's Note: This is a work of fiction.
Names, characters, places, and incidents are a
product of the author's imagination. Locales and
public names are sometimes used for
atmospheric purposes. Any resemblance to
actual people, living or dead, or to businesses,
companies, events, institutions, or locales is
completely coincidental.

Come For Fun/ Melisa Poche. -- 1st ed.
Xplicit Press, an imprint of TLM Media LLC

ISBN-13: 978-1-62327-538-9
ISBN-10: 1-62327-538-5
eISBN: 978-1-62327-590-7

Printed in the United States of America

CONTENTS

CONTENTS

1 A FLICK OF FUN

I'd never been to a movie theater by myself, but I'd been looking forward to seeing the new spy thriller by my favorite director for months. My husband had been putting if off for so long that it was about to go out of theatres.

"Babe, please. I really want to see it," I'd said, standing in front of him. I leaned over him and gave him an easy view of my warm breasts, which were proudly on display thanks to my new crimson lace push up bra. My nipples underneath were erect and craved to be caressed. Joe had been working the night shift for weeks, and we hadn't spent any time together in a long time. I wanted to see the movie, and I wanted to fuck him, so I'd spent hours getting ready in the hopes that I'd get to do both.

"Sorry honey, I'm just so drained," he said, his eyes glued on the game on TV. "Here's a twenty, why don't you find a friend to go with instead?" I grabbed the money begrudgingly and stormed out, swaying my round hips dramatically as I walked. At the door, I looked back to see if the tight swath of my black pencil skirt in his face had caught his attention. He lifted a hand in a light wave, still not looking away.

I slammed the door and walked to the car, determined to have fun one way or another.

The theater was a cinematic ghost town since this particular flick had been out for months, so I had my pick of seats. I slid into a plush seat near the back, in the middle of the aisle. The lights soon dimmed, and I sighed as I let the familiar flash of lights and Dolby surround sound wash over my over-dressed body.

As the opening credits began to roll, a person slid into the seat beside me. For a moment, my heart skipped a beat thinking that Joe had changed his mind and come to surprise me in a romantic gesture. I turned to face him, but it wasn't Joe. While Joe's face was familiar, tired and worn, this man's face was chiseled, with carefully groomed facial stubble that seems to highlight the manly ruggedness of his features.

I turned back to the movie, but couldn't stop thinking about this stranger to my left. I looked around the dim room at the rows upon rows of empty velveteen chairs. There were more than a hundred empty seats, why had he chosen to sit beside me?

Suddenly, I got a clue as I felt a rough, cool hand caress my leg. I looked over, ready to tell the stranger to fuck off, but he looked straight ahead with an indifferent expression. It was titillating, and I could feel an ache in my pussy as my long-forgotten juices began to flow, moistening the surface of my lace thong.

As the movie picked up speed, with lights flashing and heavy-bass music pumping, the man's hand worked its way deeper under my skirt. He was teasing me so forcefully that I squirmed in my seat and gripped the plastic cup holders to stop myself from writhing. Then, without warning, his fingers were inside me, urgently penetrating my wet pussy while his thumb rolled over my clit. I moaned loudly. He rubbed me harder, bringing me so close to the edge that I was ready to explode in my seat.

Suddenly, the loud, intense scene on the screen turned somber and quiet. He pulled his hand out of me and sat back in his seat, casually licking my juices off of his fingers and watching the movie.

In the quiet, I could hear my own panting and tried to calm myself. I was so close, why did he stop? I looked to him pleadingly and got my answer.

The handsome stranger had unbuckled the fly on his crisp, freshly-ironed jeans. I could see the mound of his dick plump and waiting to be released. I looked at him: "What do you want me to do?" I whispered in his ear.

"Try not to touch me. I dare you," he whispered back, his breath hot in my ear.

He was teasing me, which normally would drive me crazy with anger, but with my pussy dripping in my seat it only made me want him more. I tried to play his game. I tried to look nonchalant and pretended to turn my attention back to the movie. I had no idea what was going on, but the action on screen had taken a sharp and sexy turn, with the star receiving juicy oral in an almost full-frontal scene. It was too much. I slid my hand onto his lap and uncoiled the stranger's cock into my hand.

"Faster," he whispered urgently into my ear as my small hand slid up and down his cock. He leaned back and let out a sigh so loud that a group of teen girls sitting up front turned around and gave us a "be quiet" glare. I smiled and shrugged, trying to keep our sexy game under wraps.

I looked down at my activity and admired my work. I love the way a cock looks engorged with desire, the way the veins push against the skin. For a moment, I thought nostalgically about the last time I saw Joe's member like this, but quickly banished the thought. "He told me to have fun," I told myself.

Before long, stroking the stranger's beautiful cock wasn't enough for me, and the ache inside me had become too strong. I pushed up my skirt and start to touch myself. I was so wet that it was hard to keep my fingers in the right spot.

The stranger noticed my move and grabbed both my wrists. We stared at each other for a moment. Even in the dark, I could see that his eyes were an unusual emerald green and, despite his inexplicably aggressive behavior, there was a warmth and tenderness behind them that made me want him more.

The moment passed, and the next thing I knew his face was in my lap.

He slid my thong to my feet and flicked his tongue into my clit like it was a peach cobbler. I could feel the familiar tingly feeling of cumming begin to creep from my feet, but he frustratingly maintained steady in his rhythm.

I dug my nails into the soft cotton of his shirt: I wanted so badly to scream, to tell him to fuck me, but the poppity-pop of machine gun fire on the movie screen reminded me of where I was. I leaned down. "Please, make me cum. I need to cum now," I said.

He immediately stopped.

"No!" I said, not able to contain my frustration. The stranger zipped up his fly, grabbed my damp panties from the floor, and pulled my roughly out of my seat.

"You said you wanted to cum. Well, I want to fuck you first," he said.

"Oh," I said. "Well, okay." I followed him out of the theater, barely noticing the confused looks on the other patrons' faces."

Outside the theater, the day had turned to night and the parking lot of dark and chilly.

"Where do you want to go?" I asked as the wind blew gently up my skirt and tickled my throbbing pussy.

"Follow me," he said.

The car ride was probably the most seductive drive of my life, and I was all alone. I tried my best to focus on the road, but I kept flashing back to the dark theater and the feel of the stranger's hand on me. Smiling, I found my fingers grazing over my lap at each stop light. I used the power setting to open all of the windows - it was getting hot inside my Civic.

We'd been driving for a few minutes and I was getting nervous as I noticed that we were approaching my neighborhood. The stranger stopped in front of a house on the street behind mine. I parked my car on the street and got out, agitated.

"What the fuck is this?" I asked, both confused and turned on.

The stranger ignored me, and unlocked the front door. He walked in and, without closing the door, started taking off his clothes and walking up the stairs to the second floor of the house. I wasn't sure what to do, but I did know that I couldn't resist whatever was going on upstairs. I walked in, closed the door, and followed him upstairs and into the bedroom.

The room was minimalist and masculine, with a huge canopy bed in the middle of the room. I admired the giant bay window that streamed in blinding moon-and-starlight from outside. What a dream this was.

Once inside, the stranger ravished me. He tore off my blouse and unhooked my bra in one smooth motion. I ran my hands up his taut back as he bit and sucked my nipples.

"Isn't it so much better to be alone?" He said.

"Who are you? I replied, though I wasn't sure I wanted him to tell me as much as I wanted him to show me.

I tried to step out of my tight skirt, but tripped and fell onto my hands and knees on the bed. In an instant, the stranger was behind me. He shoved my skirt up around my waist and slid inside me.

"Holy fuck," I gasped. As much as I'd been dying to get fucked, the stranger's cock was larger than Joe and my pussy was out of practice.

The stranger ignored me, sliding his cock slowly in and out of me until I warmed up to the motion. I bucked against him, loving the feeling of being stuffed and desired. He reached around my waist and pressed down on my clit, and finally it was enough. I screamed as I came hard, my pussy convulsing, pulsating against his dick. Waves of pleasure washed over my body, and I collapsed face first on the bed.

The stranger kissed my neck softly. "Did you cum?" he asked.

"Oh, fuck yes," I said, my face mashed into the silky blue of his comforter.

"Good," he said. "Now it's my turn." He pulled his still hard cock out of me and flipped me over on the bed, pushing my legs behind my head. Sliding inside me, the stranger fucked me hard, using my legs like handlebars, for what seemed like forever. My pussy was still contracting from my earlier release, but it felt so good. Gradually, I felt the familiar urgency creep back into my pussy.

"Cum inside me," I screamed. I wanted his warm semen fill me. He said nothing but moaned and fucked me harder and faster.

"I'm going to cum. Now!" I yelled. With a final thrust, the stranger did as I asked and shot load after load inside me.

We collapsed on the bed, panting.

"Fucking pervert," the stranger said.

"What? You came onto me!" I said, indignantly pulling the blankets around me. He laughed and kissed me as he got up and moved to close the curtains.

"Not you. My neighbor in the house behind me. I just caught him watching us."

I looked up through the window and saw through the trees the back of a house. My house. Standing naked in the window with a can of Miller in one hand and his dick in the other was my husband, Joe.

The reality of Joe's silhouette shook me out of my ecstasy.

"I have to go," I said, pulling on my clothes faster than I had taken them off.

"Wait... when will I see you again?" the stranger asked. He looked a little hurt, which surprised me, considering the way we had met.

"You're new in town?"

"Yes... how did you know? I don't usually do things like this, but I didn't know anyone here and when I saw you all alone, I couldn't resist."

"Well, let's just say I think we'll be

seeing more of each other. We're neighbors." I said, walking out the door and down the stairs.

I drove home, horrified at what Joe was going to do and say. I'd never cheated on him before, and I felt terrible for betraying our vows. But then, as I put my key in the front door, I couldn't help but catch a whiff of the stranger's scent on my hand and I felt intoxicated. I wanted more.

I walked into the dark house.

"Joe?" I called, cautiously. I thought about the best way to apologize. I was sure that I could reason with my husband, if only I could find him. I noticed a light on upstairs. Swallowing the knot in my stomach and the lump in my throat, I went up.

"Babe," I said. "Are you home?"

I walked into my bedroom and found Joe laying on the bed staring at the ceiling. He was fully dressed now, and lay with his legs crossed. He seemed more relaxed than I'd seen him in months. He smiled at me and sat up.

"Hey honey, how was the movie?" He asked.

"Fine... how was your night?" I replied,

waiting for him to strike.

"Good, good. I think we might have a new neighbor."

"Oh..."

"Yeah, I saw someone moving into the house behind us. Seems like a good guy. Maybe I'll invite him over for a beer next weekend." Joe coughed.

"Er. Okay." I looked at my husband, trying to find an ounce of vengeance or malice on his face. He seemed happy and content.

"Now, come over here, babe," he said, patting the bed beside him. "I know it's been hard lately with me working so much, but I'm feeling really horny tonight, and I know you've been too. Come here."

I sat on the bed with relief, and kissed him gently. He grabbed my breast and slid his hand up my leg. I sighed, almost crying with relief. I let him take over me, and smiled as he began our usual routine. He kissed my neck, then my collarbone, then he walked his fingers slowly up my skirt, drawing teasing circles with his thumb until he reached my pussy. As he did, he suddenly stopped.

"Babe," he said with alarm. "Why aren't you wearing any underwear?"

2 COME ANYTIME
A Flick Of Fun Part 2

"Things have sure gotten more interesting since Mark moved in!" my husband, Joe, said to me, as he pulled random articles of clothing from our shared closet and threw them on the bed.

Indeed, I thought, things had been a lot different since Mark moved into the house behind ours - but not for the reasons Joe was thinking of.

Mark was the new morning sports reporter for our local cable news station. He was strikingly handsome in the way that people on television often are. His features were so chiseled that, in certain lights, he looked like a pinnacle of attractiveness - like a walking photoshop. Joe enjoyed Mark's company because he was funny and suave and knew everything about sports. In the month since Mark had moved to Oregon, Mark and Joe had spent countless afternoons drinking beer and hanging out. What Joe didn't know was that every evening when he left to work the late shift, Mark and I were fucking like the world was ending.

"I mean, we never would have thought to throw an ironic-themed costume party. Mark's just... he's just so cool," Joe said, as he held up a shirt to his chest.

"More like, Mark's hot," I whispered under my breath. Maybe it was the guilt, but I couldn't help but feeling weird about Joe's man-crush on my lover.

"What was that, hun?" Joe asked, confused.

"I said, 'it's going to be hot,'" I replied, smiling. "Maybe you should go with the short sleeves."

"Good point babe. I think I'm going to go as Tiger Woods."

I smiled at Joe, grabbed some clothes and stepped into the bathroom to get dressed for the party in private. Ever since Mark and I had met in a chance encounter at the movies, I'd started to become more aware of my sexuality, my sex appeal. Joe had been basically ignoring me for months, and now it was my time to look sexy for a man who would appreciate it.

I chose my outfit carefully, starting with my lingerie. I pulled on my new black satin bra and matching garter belt, to which I attached silky smooth stockings - purposefully neglecting to don any panties. Slipping on my smooth underthings, I couldn't help but start thinking about how Mark would take them off.

I closed my eyes and imagined Mark's big, confident hands caressing my curves, running his fingers over my body. Within seconds, I was wet just thinking about it and I found my hand reaching for my pussy giving it a pet in anticipation.

"Babe, are you taking a shower?" Joe yelled at me through the locked door.

I stopped what I'm doing and smiled. "Yes, I think I'll take a quick shower..."

I turned on the little radio that Joe keeps in the shower and scanned the stations until I found a sexy beat. Looking in the mirror, I started to dance, tentatively at first, as I watched myself undress. I removed my inky silk bra and garter slowly. A month before, I remembered morosely telling a friend that I thought I looked more like 41 than 31. But then, watching my naked body sway to the beat, I thought, "I could pass for 21. They should bottle Mark's cum and sell it at Sephora."

I stepped into the shower let the warm water run over my body like I hoped Mark's mouth would later that night. The beads of water pounded on my chest and stomach. I turned and let it gently massage my back. It was almost too much. I took the shower head off of its cradle and closed my eyes, softly moving the spray lower and lower down my torso.

The spray hit my clit and for a moment, the pressure was so intense that I had to move it away. Then, I thought above Mark's tongue swirling over my hood, and I wanted it bad. I lay down in the tub and aimed the spray over my pussy, sighing as it pounded jets of pleasure into my pussy. After a while, I changed the setting from the regular spray to the targeted jet and moved the head from my clit straight into my pussy. It felt amazing, I imagined the sensation was the same as Mark's cock impaling me as it simultaneously exploded with cum inside me. Soon it was too much and I came hard, writhing in the tub as my muscles spasmed.

There was a loud knock at the door.

"Um, babe? You've been in there a while... are you almost ready? I want to leave pretty soon. I don't want to keep Mark waiting," Joe said.

"Sure, Joe. Just give me a minute to finish my hair!" I said, drying off.

"Ok, I'll text Mark and tell him you're coming."

"Yes, Joe. Good idea. Text Mark and tell him I'm coming. I'm sure he'll understand."

We arrived at Mark's place fashionably late and I was surprised by the turnout. For a guy who just moved to town, it seemed like Mark had made quite a few friends. I knew it was irrational, but I was a little jealous of the number of women bustling around him. I felt a pang of insecurity twist in my stomach.

I was dressed as a sexy maid, telling Joe that it's an ironic choice because I was his wife and I did all the cleaning - though in reality, I was hoping that it would turn Mark on as he mentioned one time in bed how hot he finds the fluffy, short ruffled skirts.

Joe disappeared into the house with a cracked beer in hand, looking for other men to talk to as he always did at parties, and I was left alone. I wandered around a bit by myself, navigating through the ironically-clad partygoers to find myself a glass of white wine.

I got my drink, but Mark was nowhere to be found so I decided to check out the rest of the house. Though I'd been paying Mark quite a few nighttime visits lately, we usually stayed mostly in his bedroom, and I wanted to explore.

Eventually I found myself in a quiet guest room. The room was surprisingly full of interesting artwork: beautiful sketches of nude women, surrealistic sculptures and framed photographs. I was looking at a particularly exciting picture on a table when suddenly there was a familiar hand cupping my ass and hot breath on my neck.

I turned to face Mark. "Where have you..."

He silenced me with a passionate kiss. I let myself melt into him, let him explore my mouth with his long, rough tongue. He lifted me onto the table and buried his face into the low neckline of my maid's costume. I arched my back, enjoying the attention.

"There're a lot of girls here Mark. I was worried you wouldn't find me," I said, running my fingers through his hair as he pulled my breast out and sucked on my nipple until it was hard.

"There might be a lot of girls here but I've been hard for you since I got Joe's text that you were 'coming.' I need you. Now." Mark, who was dressed sharply in a suit and tie, undid his fly and pulled out his already hard cock. "Now," he said.

I climbed off the desk and knelt in front of him. Slowly, I licked the tip of his dick, flicking my tongue around the crest. Mark's hand pulled at my ponytail, gently guiding my mouth to take more and more of him until I gagged. I sucked hard, letting Mark guide my mouth up and down his shaft - slowly at first, and then faster and faster until his muscles tensed and I knew he was close.

Suddenly, the door to the room burst open, shocking us with the bright light and the loud music from the rest of the house.

"Oh shit!" A man's drunken voice, clearly my husband's, boomed into the room. I froze, Mark's cock still rapidly fucking my mouth. "Mark?" Joe asked.

Mark couldn't hold it any longer. He moaned as he came, pumping my mouth full of his warm juices. I kept my position, suckling on Mark and trying to stay hidden crouched in front of him.

"Oh, shit. I'm sorry man, I was just... looking for Rogan. Dude, I'll keep looking. So sorry!" Joe said, as he stumbled out of the room.

"No problem, man. Can you just shut the door?" Mark called out after him. Joe came back and shut the door, leaving us alone - Mark with his cock hanging relaxed in front of him and me on the floor licking the semen from the corners of my mouth.

"Are you okay? That was close," Mark said, stroking my cheek.

"Would it make me a bad person if I said that I was actually a bit more turned on?" I replied.

"I think I love you," Mark said, picking me up and throwing me on the bed, his cock already partially hard again. He pushed up the fluffy ruffles of my maid's skirt.

"Hold on. I need something," Mark said. He began rummaging through the closet, eventually emerging with a large feather duster. "I think this belongs to you."

Mark knelt down in front of my and brushed the soft feathers over my pussy. He ran the feathers in tantalizing swirls, and I felt myself getting wetter and wetter. Soon, the tips of the feathers were wilting from my juices.

"Fuck me," I whispered, urgently.

Mark took away the feather duster and stood up, revealing his once again hard dick. He leaned over me, but instead of plunging himself into me, he took the handle of the duster and used it to gently explore my pussy.

"I wanna watch you," he said, fucking me with the handle with one hand, while stroking himself with the other. He toyed with me until I was twisting in pleasure, then he threw the duster to the ground and mounted me. Mark plunged his cock inside me and I almost swallowed it with my pussy.

"Yes, fuck. I've been dreaming about your hard dick inside me all day. Make me cum!" I yelled, bucking my hips against him. He grabbed my hands and pinned them over my head, closing his eyes, concentrating on fucking me as hard as possible. He plunged so deep inside me that I thought he might impale me. As I got closer, I reached down and rubbed my clit frantically until I exploded with cum. As my pussy contracted against his cock, Mark came too. Still convulsing, I grabbed his balls and pulled gently down, massaging them until his whole supply was emptied onto my stomach.

We sat silently on the bed for a few moments as we came down. Then, without warning, Mark started laughing uncontrollably.

"What's so funny?" I said, confused and a bit hurt.

"I'm sorry, Rogan," he said. "It's just that... well... you wore the perfect costume for a moment like this. Look at your belly. There's a real mess to clean up."

Back at the party, I found my morose husband drinking alone in the kitchen. He didn't notice me at first, so I took a moment to observe him. Seated on one of the kitchen chairs was Joe, sweet and kind but so unsatisfying. Joe was a good man, and I loved him, but ever since Mark had come into the picture, things had been so much more interesting. I wondered how much longer I could keep up the charade, but I knew that telling Joe the truth would only do him more harm than good. It was in his best interest that I kept things quiet.

Mark walked up behind me, slyly slapping my ass as he walked into the kitchen and patted Joe on the shoulder.

"Cheer up, man. It's a party. And look, I found your wife."

"Rogan, where have you been?" Joe

slurred.

"Just, cleaning up the mess," I said.

Mark smiled and handed me the feather duster from our sexcapades. "Rogan, this must be yours - very nice costume, by the way. I've always had a thing for maids."

"Don't get any funny ideas," I said, a bit nervous that Joe would pick up on his cheekiness. I rubbed the feathers of the duster in Mark's face playfully, being sure to let him feel the lingering dampness from my pussy on the feathers. Joe didn't seem to notice and began gathering up the remaining beers we had.

"Dude, it's been a fun time, but I think I've had one too many. I'm going to take Rogan home before she gets too bored, she hates things like this." Joe said wryly, limply grabbing my hand. But maybe you could come over tomorrow for the game? Our place? I'll try to convince my wife to wear her cute costume while she waits on us."

"Sure man," Mark said. "I think I'd enjoy that more than you'd know, being new to town and all. And Rogan?"

I turned and gave Mark one last lustful look.

"I just want you to know that you can come anytime."

3 PEEP SHOW
A Flick Of Fun Part 3

The first thing I noticed when I woke up was how Joe breathed. Even before I opened my eyes, I could hear him wheezing. Every few seconds it was a slow whistle, like sitting on a pool toy with a hole in it. I pulled the comforter over my ears and tried to drown out the sound and think of something other than the husband who had been growing more and more aggravating to me over the past few months.

Cozy in my early morning haze, I began to think about my lover and new neighbor, Mark. Mark's firm body glistening in the shower. Mark's piercing green eyes gazing intensely down on me in the moonlight as he fucked me in the night. Mark sleeping softly, silently in my arms. I grew wet thinking about it. Still safe under the cocoon of my blankets, I reached under my side of the bed and pulled out a small pink vibrator and switched it on to hear its familiar hum.

I rubbed the gentle buzz over the lips of my pussy, allowing it to massage me awake. I pinched my nipples, drawing my large breasts to my lips and licking the tip as Mark would do. I placed the toy over my clit, turning the setting up a few notches until the vibration was so intense that I could feel it reverberate through my toes.

I stretched out on the bed, sighing, forgetting for a moment where I was and who I was with. Then, Joe's heavy arm flopped over me and brought me back to reality. I quietly switch off my toy and slipped out of bed, eager to escape the monotony of my marital bed.

Downstairs in the kitchen, I made coffee and turned on the television. I'd never been one for sports, but Mark was the new sports reporter on our local TV news morning program, and I loved to watch him in his element.

Soon enough, the sports segment came on and there he was. Even on the small screen, I could practically smell his sex oozing through the glass. I loved how intense he was, sharply dressed in a gray pinstripe suit and bright green tie. He bantered with the program's anchor, Lisa Ray, with so much charisma that you could see on her face that she was enamored with him. I felt a surge of jealousy bubble under my skin.

"Morning, babe. Tough shift last night. I'm exhausted. Make me some food?" Joe sauntered into the kitchen.

I didn't feel like talking, but silently started assembling the ingredients for an omelet for Joe, without taking my eyes off the screen, off of Mark and Lisa. Joe followed my gaze.

"Man, that Lisa Ray's beautiful, eh? I bet Mark loves working with her," Joe said. I pretended to ignore him, but Joe persisted. "Like, wow. If we had girls like that at the factory, I don' know if I'd get any work done."

I dropped the eggs and stormed out of the kitchen, leaving behind a bewildered Joe to finish his own breakfast.

I spent the rest of the morning back in the comfort of our bed, sulking. Around noon, I got a text message from Mark. "Hey, gorgeous. I'm home, come over for an afternoon delight?" I was conflicted. The mere sound of his text alert made me feel like Pavlov's dog - wet and ready to fuck. And yet, I couldn't help but feel jealous and guilty. If Mark was cheating with me, how could I tell he wasn't cheating on me? And the more I felt jealous about cheating with Mark, the worse I felt about cheating on Joe. I ignored the message, throwing the phone under the table.

Half an hour later, Mark had sent me several persistent messages that I left unanswered. Eventually, he stood in his window where I could see him, our bedrooms facing each other. He grinned his sexy smile and it was almost enough for me to melt. But I couldn't shake my dark feelings.

There was a knock at the door and Joe walked tentatively in, a look of concern on his soft, spongy face.

"Babe, I think I know why you're mad. I haven't been paying enough attention to you, and then I start going off about how hot Lisa Ray is...I'm really sorry. I don't know what I was thinking, because to me, you're the most beautiful woman in the world."

I softened a bit, and then I caught a glimpse of Mark watching us through the window. I was turned on.

"Seriously, babe," Joe continued, oblivious to Mark's visuals, "Let me show you how much I love you."

Joe crawled into bed beside me, and tenderly pulled my shirt over my head. He kissed my neck and down my breasts lightly - so softly that I almost couldn't feel it. Yet, as I looked out the window, I could see Mark watching in pure horror. Good, I thought. Let him watch me with someone else and feel jealous; it was his turn.

"Enough with the tenderness," I said, pushing Joe off of me and ripping off my pants. "If you want to do this, you're going to make me cum."

Joe was speechless. I'd never been this forward with him in bed. Still, I could see his dick hardening underneath his sweatpants. With one eye on the window, I guided Joe's face into my lap. "Lick it."

At first, Joe was hesitant. He hadn't eaten my pussy since we got married ten years ago - he probably forgot what it tasted like. "Mmm..." I moaned. He might have been out of practice, but I was so turned on watching Mark watch me that my senses seemed heightened.

"Right there. Lick it harder," I said,

pushing his tufty, sandy blonde head harder into my crotch. Joe did as he was told, gripping my thighs while moving his tongue in mechanical swirls over my clit. He clutched my ass, lifting my hips up so that he could delve deeper into me with his tongue.

In the window, I could see Mark pulling his cock out of his suit pants and begin to stroke his cock. "Oh, yeah," I moaned.

Joe looked up as I spoke, and caught a glimpse of the window. He froze. "What the fuck is going on?"

I couldn't move, caught in a precarious position. "Nothing's going on."

Joe looked up at Mark, who stood frozen in place as well in his window.

"You want a show for Mark? You have a little crush on my friend, eh?" Joe was angry, but didn't seem to have figured out the depth of my deceit. I stayed silent. "Let's give him a show then."

Joe pushed me onto the bed and pulled off his pants, revealing his cock which was the hardest I'd ever seen it. I spread my legs in the usual missionary position that Joe had always loved. Instead, he sat with his back against the headboard and pulled me onto his lap. "Ride me," he said.

I lowered myself onto my husband's stiff cock. I turned around to see that Mark was indeed still watching us, then I began to ride Joe. I bounced up and down, surprised at how good it felt as I pushed Joe deeper and deeper inside me. Joe pushed my breasts into his face, biting down onto my nipples until they were sore. Then he pushed me off of him and onto my back, shoving his cock between my breasts. I squeezed them together and let him fuck my tits, using my pussy juice as lubricant. Joe groaned and looked up at the window. "You like that, buddy? You like how I fuck my wife?" Joe seemed to get a lot of pleasure out of this voyeurism. I decided to try to take control of the situation once again.

I grabbed Joe's cock and started to suck it feverishly, licking his balls, up his shaft, then shoving the whole thing into my mouth. Joe seemed thrown off by my aggression and was still for a moment. Before long though, he got into it, and was happily pumping his cock into my face.

I couldn't believe how turned on I was by my long-docile husband. When he flipped me over onto my hands and knees, I shook my ass eagerly in anticipation.

"Okay Rogan, I'm going to fuck you now, and I'm going to fuck you hard. But I want you to stare at Mark while I do. Watch him while I fuck you, okay?" Joe said.

Before I could answer, Joe's dick thrust into my pussy. He grabbed my hair as reigns and fucked me from behind, pulling on it hard so that I was forced to look up at Mark as he fucked me. I could still see Mark through the window but now he was totally stripped waist down and unabashedly jerking off. Behind me, I could hear Joe grunt as he got closer and closer to finishing.

In the window, Mark jerked faster and faster, stroking his big cock until it exploded, covering the bay window with splashed of cum that looked like starbursts of sex. He moved back into the shadows, and then it was just Joe and me.

Before I knew what was happening, Joe started bucking harder and faster against me, then I felt a warm liquid shooting onto my back. He moaned with pleasure and slapped my ass, falling off me, he lay, panting, on the bed.

"Now," Joe said. "You want to finish? Why don't you use that little toy you keep under the bed."

I never knew that Joe knew about my vibrator. I wondered what else he knew, but my pussy was aching so hard to come I decided to do as I was told. I reached under the bed and switched the toy on. My pussy was already raw from fucking, but I forced myself to allow the vibrator to shake my insides.

Beside me on the bed, Joe lazily stroked his cock. "Make yourself come," he said and I did as I was told. I turned it on to maximum speed and shoved the vibrator deep inside my vagina, and stroked my clit with my fingers. I rubbed faster, but I couldn't seem to come. Frustrated, I felt a tear stream down my cheek. Joe wiped the tear away.

"You were a pretty big talker earlier," he said. "Why can't you come now?"

"Please Joe," I pleaded. "Help me come." I looked into my husband's eyes, searching for a glimpse of the love we'd once had when we were young. He softened.

Without a word, Joe climbed on top of me. He pulled the vibrator out of my pussy and held it against my clit. He kissed me tenderly and deeply, and like magic, I felt my body begin to shake. Starting at my toes, I felt a warm sensation move up my body, reaching my fingertips as I convulsed against my husband's body.

As I finished cumming, Joe collapsed against me. We lay still for hours until we fell into a deep sleep. As I drifted off, I thought I caught a glimpse of Mark watching us from his window, but the thought of Mark seemed to dissipate as I fell asleep in my husband's arms.

When I woke up on Sunday morning, I knew it was over with Mark, and I felt amazing. Being with Mark had made life more exciting but knew it turned me into a person that I didn't really like very much.

I looked over at Joe, who was sleeping peacefully and for the first time in a long time – silently, beside me. I kissed the tip of his nose softly and his eyelids fluttered open. "Good morning, Joe," I said. He looked up at me and smiled.

"I just wanted to say that yesterday was amazing. I haven't felt this close to you in so long... it was really great," I said.

Joe looked at me for a long time, tracing the features of my face with his thick fingers.

"Babe, last night was great," Joe said. "So great, that I think we need to talk about Mark."

I was terrified. Did he know? Was last night a pity fuck before he left me? I felt my lip begin to quiver: just as I realized that Joe was the one all along, was he going to divorce me? "What about Mark, Joe?"

"Rogan, let's be honest here: I think you already know what I'm going to say," he said.

"Maybe... please, Joe. Just say it."

"Well, babe, the thing is, ever since Mark moved into our neighborhood, I've noticed a certain sexual energy charging, and last night just confirmed how on track I was."

I began to cry. "No..."

"Yes, babe. Yesterday when I was fucking you, watching him... I think we might have had a moment. Mark and I just get along so well and really hit it off. And when I saw him cum, I came harder than I ever have before."

"Wait, what are you saying Joe?"

"Rogan, babe. I think the reason things have been so stagnant between us in bed lately, might be because I'm more attracted to someone like, well, Mark. Don't get me wrong, I still love you. I just think I might love him too. So, what you do you think? Would you ever consider fucking... both of us?"

.

4 SWEET BUT NOT SACCHARINE

I never thought I'd find a better place to inject cream than my cakes, until the day I hired Tom.

As the owner of Cake Queen's Confectionary, I'd spent most of my days for the past several years completely dedicated to making the tastiest baked goods possible, and things were going exceptionally well. What had started out as just me baking in my basement had expanded into a mid-town storefront. After my strawberry cheesecake cake bites were featured in the dining section of the newspaper, business exploded. I needed to hire a decorator to help keep up with demand, so I placed an ad online.

I received hundreds of applications and wasn't looking forward to interviewing. I'm naturally shy and liked working by myself. I was insecure and afraid that the candidates would see through my façade of confidence and walk out.

Still, I mustered up the courage and held interviews. There was Mary, a plump middle-aged woman with experience sifting flour. There was Sara, a college student who'd watched a few too many cupcake shows on TV and had no experience. And there was Tom: a trained baker with a passion for cake design. He brought me a small, delicately assembled cupcake adorned with airy blue fondant that looked like the sky. I was hooked.

Interviewing Tom, I tried to keep things professional—he was by far the most qualified candidate and I didn't want to lose him. But it was hard to stay focused, as I kept finding myself tuning him out, mesmerized by the pillows of his lips as he talked. Tom's lips looked soft and were a mauvey pink; they looked like he had just sucked on a juicy cherry popsicle. Dark curls framed his face, their gentle curves offsetting the hulk of his muscular build. I wondered if he tasted as good as he looked.

"So, the thing is, I'm really passionate about baking. I've been working in these busy grocer's bakeries the past few years, and the operations are just too big—my skills aren't being utilized frosting a million white slab cakes a week. I want to work somewhere more... intimate. Somewhere where I can really grow. And I think you might just be it," Tom said, smiling broadly.

I opened my mouth to speak, but was too startled to talk. Instead, I nodded and nervously tossed my long blonde hair over my shoulder.

"So, does that mean I have it?" Tom asked, practically vibrating with excitement.

"Yes, you've got me," I squeaked, blushing. "I mean, you've got the job. Can you start tomorrow at 5?"

Tom's first day of work was spectacular. Being self-taught as a baker, I'd never worked in a kitchen with someone else before. We quickly fell into a rhythm, moving in and out and around each other. It was seductive, like a dance. As I stepped behind him, I found myself getting just a little closer than necessary, brushing my breasts against his back. As I bent over to form lavender lattice work on a cake, Tom slid behind me with a tray of pastries—and I swore I could feel a firmness from his hips push ever-so-slightly into my ass. He lingered for a moment, pressing his cock into my back faintly, but surely, as he leaned over my shoulder. "Gorgeous, Anna. Maybe you can teach me that technique sometime."

I was flustered and excited but tried to maintain a sense of professionalism to mask my delight.

The rest of the day only worked me up more and more. When customers arrived, Tom and I took turns serving them. I liked to hang back of the shop: half prepping cakes and half watching the firmness of Tom's ass whenever he bent over to pull things out of the bottom shelf of the display case for customers.

By the end of the day, I was ready to burst. "So, Tom. How was it for you today?" I blurted as we closed up that evening. I felt myself blush and busied myself with wiping down the counter with a damp cloth.

"Today was amazing," he said, looking into my eyes. He placed his hand over mine. "I think I found just what I've been looking for here." He winked, grabbed his bag, and walked out the door. I watched him walk out, speechless.

Over the next few weeks, things in the shop got busier and busier, and I got more and more horny. Tom's handsome face was like free advertising, as women from the surrounding area spilled in — jeopardizing their waistlines for a chance to interact with Tom's charm and taste his delicious cream puffs.

I was insanely attracted to him, but the increased workload took up so much of my time that it became easy to be a fairly chaste boss — although I did take every chance I got to press my body against his whenever the opportunity arose.

After a particular busy Sunday rush, Tom and I were exhausted. We closed up shop at a languid pace, chatting and laughing more than we were cleaning.

"So what made you get into baking?" I asked Tom.

"There's just something so sexy about it. I love mixing sumptuous ingredients together to make something that people put in their mouths. I love making things beautiful and then licking them apart and swallowing them," he said. Tom moved closer to me as he spoke.

"That's what makes working here so perfect. I get to work on beauty, and with beauty," he said.

I laughed. "You're really into cake, Tom."

"I'm here for more than the cake." Tom was barely an inch away from me; I couldn't help but inhale his breath. Slowly, he leaned down and kissed me, softly at first. Then, his tongue was in my mouth, flicking at my tongue, greedily stealing the air straight from my lungs. He dropped the broom he'd been holding and grabbed my breasts: his hands were so big that he could cup my entire D cup in his palm. I could feel my panties dampen beneath my gray baker's pants.

I pulled away, wanting nothing more than to fuck him, but worried about the implications. I was his boss, and I needed him to make my business succeed.

"Tom..." I began.

He smiled at me. "I know, I know. You're my boss. But I couldn't resist," he said. "You should see how sexy you look right now."

I squirmed, resisting the urge to jump on him.

"I better go. Goodnight, Anna," he said. He walked backwards out the door with a grin on his face and a huge erection clear and proud tenting his pants.

The next morning, I went to work, determined to have a talk with Tom about professionalism. I'd worked so hard to make Cake Queen a success, and I couldn't lose it now for some fling. Even if it was an incredibly sexy fling.

I was kneading some fondant for a slab cake when Tom arrived. He didn't say a word but stared at my cleavage, which was visible from beneath my thin black tank top as I leaned over my work. He walked behind me and put his arms around me, his hands over mine.

"Teach me your technique, Anna," he said. His body was so warm behind me; I felt like I was melting into him. I kneaded the fondant, and Tom's body moved in sync with mine. Each time I moved forward into the knead, he pushed his hips closer to mine. Soon, the lump pressing against my ass was unmistakable.

Tom kissed my neck, sucking hard on my milky flesh. His hands moved up my arms and then pulled my shirt over my head and unhooked my bra. I turned around.

"Tom, we can't do this!" I said, crossing my arms over my now-naked chest.

"Okay," he said, moving back and looking hurt. "I'm sorry Anna, I thought this was what you wanted. He turned around and started pulling baking pans from the shelf. "I'll just get to work then."

I watched him for a moment before I noticed that my hand was gripping my pussy over my pants. "Fuck it," I said, running over to him and kissing him hard on the lips.

Tom took the hint. He pulled his T-shirt and pants off, revealing the huge cock that I had long suspected hid beneath. I stepped out of my pants so that we were both totally naked. We explored each other's bodies with our hands and tongues.

"Wait," he said. I stood confused — my pussy dripping wet with desire — in the middle of the kitchen as Tom rushed around. He put a dab of yellow buttercream on the shaft of his dick. "Come and taste my creation."

I knelt in front of Tom and lapped the frosting off of his cock. He moaned. I licked every saccharine bit and then put the entire shaft in my mouth. I moved my lips up and down, sucking hard. Tom only seemed to grow at my touch. I grabbed his cool balls and massaged them—it was too much for him.

Tom pulled me up and lifted me onto

the counter, spreading my legs wide. "Now I'm hungry," he said slyly. He took a canister of whipped cream and sprayed it over my pussy. The cold cream hitting my hot pussy made me tingle, and the spray created a fluffy mound in my crotch. Tom bent down, his hands keeping my knees spread wide and slowly lapped up the cream. With each lick, his tongue got closer and closer to my clit. Soon, he was sucking on my clit; I looked down, surprised by how puffy it looked as he pulled away. My clit seemed to grow to get closer to him. I moaned and arched my back.

Tom stood up, placing the tip of his stick-straight dick at the crest of my pussy. "Do you want it?" he teased.

I looked at him, no longer shy or worried about my career; all I wanted was for him to pound himself into me. "I need you to fuck me, right now, and fill my mouth with your cream," I said.

It was all he needed to hear. Tom thrust into me. I wailed at the sensation as his huge dick stretched my insides. "Fuck, yes Tom!"

He picked me up, and I clung to him as he bounced her up and down on his dick. "Oh my god, that's so deep," I said, my arms gripping around his neck. The change in angle felt amazing, and I could feel myself verging closer and closer to coming. I dug my nails into Tom's back. He bounced me faster as his fingers dug into the cheeks of my ass.

Suddenly, Tom lifted me off of him and we sat on the floor. I lay down, and Tom kissed my face and neck. He reached to the counter and pulled a jar of the chocolate drizzle we used to top the double fudge cupcakes. He drizzled it in a professional-looking swirl over each of my breasts. I reached down and rubbed my clit as Tom leaned over me and licked each swirl greedily. Once my chest was completely clean, he alternated between sucking my left and right nipple until they were tender and erect.

Tom moved on top of me, shoving his cock back into my pussy. He pumped wildly, rapidly as he stared into my eyes. His breathing quickened, moving from a steady inhale to nearly a wheeze as he thrust harder into me. Finally, he was ready to cum: "Ready for a taste?" he gasped.

I nodded, kneeling in front of him and opening my mouth. He grabbed his cock and aimed its tip towards my face; he spasmed as he shot load after load of hot cum into my mouth. I swallowed the salty treat, and Tom knelt down to my level and kissed me.

Tom and I lay naked on the floor of the bakery holding hands. His fingers drew lazy circles on the skin of my stomach, and I closed my eyes dreamily.

"Well, that was certainly a treat," I said, finally. I looked over at Tom's sexy face.

"Indeed. Let's keep that one in our private menu; I'm not sure the customers could handle it," he said. I laughed.

"Should we get dressed? I guess we have to open up soon," Tom said with a sigh.

"You know what, Tom? I think today should be devoted to professional development. I really want to perfect this recipe."

Tom grinned at me and stood up to get supplies for the next batch.

5 BABY YOU CAN'T LIGHT MY FIRE

Working from home has its ups and downs. The job security can be terrible, there aren't any benefits and you miss out on a ton of water cooler chat. But, on the plus side, there's just so much more freedom: no commute, take breaks whenever you want and wear what you want. And, with my line of work, I definitely wear what I want.

You see, I'm something of a stay-at-home entrepreneur. In the last year, I transformed my apartment into a sexual fun house, fully equipped with theme rooms, props and multiple web-ready cameras. The living room was the animal room — filled with leopard-print velvet and exotic animals. The bathroom was for slippery fun, with Jacuzzi tub and a mini water slide — I fit a lot of sudsy fun in for my clients. My bedroom was the playroom: I had swings, ropes and toys. The kitchen was for fire play: I had matches and lighters to put on shows for my more adventurous clients.

Overall, working from home as a webcam worker was fun, exciting and tax free. I used my rooms and props to put together sexy solo shows for my clients — keeping myself satisfied and my bank account full.

Last week, I was having a typical morning workday: I was spread eagle on a plush gray patterned love seat in the living room putting on a show for on my regulars, Bill, a rich businessman. I'd dressed up like a naughty secretary, and had stripped to my black satin bra and thong and matching black stiletto heels.

I played with a long beaded necklace I draped my neck with. "Do you like my necklace?" I asked Bill. I pulled it off my neck and rubbed the beads over my pussy.

Bill's voice boomed from my laptop, "Oh yeah, baby, that's nice. I'm stroking myself with my necklace too."

I rubbed the beads faster and faster.

"Grab your boobs," Bill yelled. I obliged, groping my breasts and groaning while looking seductively into the webcam.

"Ohhhh yeah," Bill's voice screamed. "Thanks baby, I just came."

I smiled. "Great! Same time next week? Your card will be charged later on tonight," I said. I threw on my white blouse and signed off of the computer.

I was just about to log in with another client when there was a knock at the door. For one year that I'd lived in that apartment, I'd never had anyone but the mailman come to my door. Intrigued, I opened it.

"Good morning, Miss. Annual fire inspection." A dark-haired man stood at my door in full fireman regalia holding a clipboard.

The fireman looked me up and down, taking in my sexy black underthings swathing my tight body. "Am I... interrupting something?" he deducted.

"No, I just work from home," I said casually, trying to hold the door as closed as possible behind my back. "What can I do for you?"

"Did you see the notice in the mailroom? It's the annual fire inspection. I just need to do a sweep of your apartment, test your alarms and make sure there are no hazards to report," he said while staring openly at my breasts.

Shit. I didn't let anyone into my apartment because I didn't want anyone to find out about my telecommuting occupation: not only was it my own business, but I didn't exactly report my income on my taxes. Also, I was a bit concerned about what this fireman might think of my fire play kitchen set up. I decided to try and distract him.

"Oh! No, I must have missed the notice, so sorry!" I said, playing with my beaded necklace over my tits. "Is it really necessary? The place is just a mess and I don't really like to let anyone in."

He broke his gaze from my boobs, and tried to look past me into the apartment. "I'm sorry, but yes — it has to happen now. It's the law, and if you don't oblige I'm going to have to report you. It could end up escalating pretty far... a pretty girl like you doesn't want to deal with all that, do you? Don't worry about any mess." The fireman pushed his way past me and into my apartment.

"Oh. My. God," he said. "What are you doing in here?" He stepped into the kitchen and looked at the candles, lighters and fire toys. "This is a recipe for disaster! I'm sorry, but I have to report this." He got out his clipboard and started writing something.

"No!" I grabbed the clipboard from his hand. "Don't worry about this, you just haven't had a tour of the place. Let me show you around."

I led the fireman - who had a name tag on his jacket that identified him as "Rick" - into the living room.

"What's with these animals?" he said, looking around at the monkey and snake I had caged. "THIS can't be legal either. You're hot, lady, but you're a fucking freak."

I pushed him onto the couch and straddled him. "You could say that," I said. "But wouldn't you rather I show you how much of a freak I can be?" I took off his fireman's jacket and shirt. I unhooked my bra so that we our chests were pressed together skin to skin. Looking into his deep brown eyes, I grabbed a candle from the table behind the couch, and dripped a few drops of warm wax onto our chests. Rick bit his lips, but didn't say another word, so I decided to push things a bit further.

I stood up on the couch so that I was still straddling him while still on my feet. Though the 5-inch heels of my stilettos dug into the soft surface of the couch, I swayed in front of him, and ran my pussy into his face. Rick reached up, and slipped a finger under the surface of my black panties. He started fingering me. "Oh, your pussy's so wet," he exclaimed.

I reached behind him to the table behind the couch with my work supplies, and grabbed a pair of scissors. I snipped the sides of my panties, so that they fell to the floor and it was just my naked pussy in front of his mouth. He took the hint and started licking.

Once my pussy was drenched inside and out, I took to the task of distracting fireman Rick. I slid down him, and unbuttoned his thick black pants with my teeth. I undid his fly and eased his pants down to his ankles and off his feet. I hovered my mouth over the head of his dick, which was rock hard. Just as I was about to lean down and give it a lick, I smiled at him and stood up.

"How rude of me! You're trying to do your job. Maybe we should take a look around and look for other heat... hazards?" I said.

Rick nodded and stood to follow me.

I showed Rick to my bathroom wonderland.

"See, sir?" I said, "There's no danger here, so long as we've got all this water to keep things cool and slippery, right?"

I strutted to the tub and turned it on, adding a healthy dose of sweet jasmine bubble bath. Soon, the tub was fragrant and sudsy.

I kissed Rick, slowly at first, then with more intensity. He started getting into it, and I led him to the tub. We stepped in and sat down facing each other, our legs intertwined.

"Now," I said, "I don't see any danger here, do you?"

Rick stroked my long legs under the sudsy water.

"I've really appreciated the tour, but I do see some danger. You're in real danger of getting fucked," he said, sliding me closer to him so that I was almost in his lap. He reached down and placed the tip of his cock in my pussy, then grabbed my back and pulled me to him, impaling my pussy with his dick.

The water must have made my already thin body ultra light, because Rick bounced me on his cock like I was a feather. Water splashed everywhere — the room was set up for lots of solo plays on camera, and I wasn't used to having someone else in the tub with me. Not that I would complain, as Rick's cock was deliciously hard with just the slightest curve; each bounce on him stroked my G-spot and made me want to come.

I leaned back in the water, letting my chocolate brown hair get wet. He pulled me up so we were face to face and kissed me ferociously.

Just when I thought Rick was about to come, I pulled away from him.

"One second," I said. I ran back into the living room for a second and came back with Rick's fireman hat. "I've always wanted to fuck a man in uniform. Please?"

Rick obliged, putting on the hat. He grabbed my hand, "get back in here."

"I think we're clean enough now," I said. "Why don't I finish the tour? You've really got to see the kitchen."

In the kitchen, I lit a variety of candles of all shapes and sizes and scents. In the daytime, the effect left sultry shadows on our faces and a dull but intense heat in the room.

"What do you think?" I asked, standing naked, still slightly damp from the bath, and with the lighter in hand, in the middle of the kitchen.

"I guess, sometimes a little fire isn't so bad," he said and pulled me into his arms. "Let's get cooking."

Still wearing his fireman hat, Rick kissed and licked and bit every inch of me, starting from my neck and finishing at my toes. When he was done, he leaned me against the stove and propped my leg up onto his shoulder, so that I was standing in a split. Rick slid his cock into my pussy, and with a moan, started to thrust inside me. I grabbed onto the burners behind me to steady myself, as Rick fucked hard, bucking and pumping into me.

We fucked like that for several minutes, until he lifted me up. I wrapped my arms around his neck and my legs around his back and let him fuck me in the air. In the tub, I had thought that it was the water that made me so light to carry. Now, I realized that Rick was just that strong — the muscles he'd built to carry people out of the fire had made him strong enough to fuck me in the air. This thought turned me on and I reached down with one hand to stroke my clit in rhythm with Rick's thrusts.

"Oh fuck yeah, I'm going to come," he cried.

"Let me down," I said, "come on my tits."

"No way baby," he said, through clenched teeth, squeezing his eyes, "I'm putting out your fire." With that, Rick's big cock shot a huge load inside my pussy.

As he came down, Rick put me down and I stood on the kitchen floor with droplets of his cum seeping down my leg. He walked around the apartment gathering his things.

"So," I said, "I guess I passed the inspection then?" I wiped a stray dollop of semen off of my calf. "You can just forget about what I do in the privacy of my home?"

Rick, now dressed, laughed. "Sorry babe, but just because you fucked me better than I've been fucked in years doesn't make you exempt from the rules. I'm still going to have to write you up and report you. I'm a professional."

I seethed at him for a moment, then smiled. "No, I don't think you'll be doing that, Rick," I said.

He chuckled. "Why the fuck not?"

"Well..." I said, "You never did ask me what I do in here. My place is wired with 10 live webcams... we've just given quite a show. I'm not sure how professional your boss would think you were, seeing you fuck me with your hat on.

"You bitch!" he cried.

"Well?"

Rick sighed, and picked up his clipboard. He wrote down a few notes, then tore off the bottom of the sheet of paper and handed it to me.

"Here you go — inspection passed," he said.

"Thanks, " I said, opening the door to let him out. "I can't wait for next year's inspection."

I slapped the sexy fireman on the ass and slammed the door.

6 MODEL CITIZEN

"Life's a bitch, Julia," my husband Jerry said, smiling behind me as I looked at myself in the full-length mirror in our bedroom. I looked myself up and down: at 26, my body had changed a lot since the last time I worked as a model. When I was a teen, every inch of my body was taut and tight, bronzed and lithe.

Now, after two babies, curves had popped up all over my body, filling out my breasts and ass and hips. Even in my baggy sweat suit, I could see the extra pounds. I tried to preen. At least my long, dark hair was still glossy. And, thankfully, my face was still youthful and contoured.

"I'm nervous, Jerry," I said, jumping

up and down anxiously.

"Babe, I know it's been a while, but I still think you're gorgeous. And we need the money. You've got to at least try this shoot," he said. I sighed. I knew Jerry cared more about the paycheck than he did my well-being. He'd been laid off from the plant a few weeks ago, and though he'd been offered a few jobs, he was really enjoying not going into work. It had been his idea for me to get back into modeling so that he could stay home with the kids and — despite my body confidence issues — I'd reluctantly agreed.

I sighed. "Okay, for us." Jerry pecked me on the lips. I grabbed my tote bag and left for the set.

I was shooting a swimwear feature for Modern Mom magazine — a lucky break booking from an old friend in the industry who had heard I was looking for cash.

While I was nervous about how my new voluptuous body would look on camera, I was looking forward to easing back into the modeling scene with this shoot. I was sure that a Modern Mom feature would be full of demure suits and a comforting, mommy-friendly environment.

I arrived on set to find a small warehouse decked out like a beach — a few assistants were adjusting bright lights to shine on a pile of sand that had been plopped into the middle of the room. Not what I was expecting.

"You Julia?" A no-nonsense, heavyset woman walked briskly towards me. "Here's the wardrobe. Get changed and get into makeup. We shoot in 20."

Flustered, I walked to a corner of the room to change — and was horrified by the swimsuit she had handed me. It was a skimpy, kelly-green string bikini. The top was sheer with triangle tops that looked like they'd barely cover half of my still-swollen, engorged breasts. The bottom was cut in a deep V and was gathered at the butt, so it would cling to every arc of my ass.

"Isn't this shoot for Modern Mom?" I screeched. A production assistant walking past stopped: "Yeah, it is, but the features called 'Mom's still got it: Sexy beach wear for young moms.'" I frowned; I wasn't sure I had it in me to pull out the full-on sex appeal, and I was worried that I wouldn't come off as sexy on camera. I wondered what I had gotten myself into.

"Hurry up! Makeup's ready!" The

bossy lady from before screamed at me from across the room. I found a corner with a mirror and a partial curtain that looked like it had been set up as a changing area and quickly put on the swimsuit. Once dressed, I stared at myself in the mirror, shocked.

The bikini looked amazing. The curves that I'd been so afraid of popped against the vibrant color of the fabric. The tiny top made my already large breasts look gigantic; they were so full; I couldn't help running my fingers around their sides, which only made my nipples hard and visible through the sheer Lycra. I felt a twinge in my pussy that I hadn't felt in months and tried to suppress it — I didn't want to get the borrowed bikini wet with my pussy juices.

Sitting in the makeup chair though, things didn't get much better. I watched as, for the first time in years, my tired face was shaped and highlighted into something truly beautiful. I realized, with delight, that I looked really hot.

As the makeup girl chatted on about TV shows and her alimony payments, I felt my pussy getting wetter and wetter looking at myself. When she wasn't looking, I discreetly reached a finger under the crotch of the suit and my suspicions were confirmed: it was like a bowl of sweet cream was resting inside the bikini bottom. I casually explored my wet pussy and tried to think of the last time Jerry and I had fucked: I was pretty sure it had been months, but I honestly couldn't remember.

I pulled my finger out quickly and nonchalantly licked my finger, savoring my flavor. "Oh god," I thought, "this wasn't good."

Once my makeup was done, most of the set cleared out — the only people that needed to be there for the next hour were me and the photographer, so the others went off for lunch, leaving us alone.

"So, Julia, I heard this is your first shoot in a while. I've got to say, you look fantastic," said the photographer. "I'm Alex, by the way," he said, shaking my hand.

"Hi Alex," I said, dazzled by the sexy man in front of me.

Most of the photographers I'd worked with as a teen had been delicate — and most definitely not of interest to me. Alex seemed different. He was a hulking man, about 6 feet 5, with rich dark skin and a deep, sexy voice. He was dressed smartly in an expensive-looking black sweater and crisp khaki pants. I let my hand linger in his for a moment, enjoying the roughness of his touch.

He coughed. "Ok, well, maybe we could start with you just doing some playful stuff on the beach set? Jump around a bit maybe? Think fun and free mom," he said. He turned on some deep, sensual beats on an iPod speaker to set the mood.

I climbed onto the pile of sand and danced around a bit. I was hyper -aware of how my tits jiggled with my movement. I looked into the camera, but couldn't help but notice that the more I moved, the bigger the crease in the crotch of Alex's pants grew. Pushing thoughts of my husband aside, I decided to see how far I could push the job.

I knelt in the sand and started stroking my tits seductively. "How's that?" I asked.

Alex kept snapping pictures. "Gorgeous," he said, looking away from the camera and into my eyes, licking his pillow- like lips.

I felt feisty and sexy in a way I forgot about, so I slowly moved the triangles of my bikini top aside to reveal my breasts. They were so big that I could lick my own nipples, so I did — never breaking eye contact with the camera. Alex kept snapping images with one hand, while the other trailed towards the front of his pants.

I got on my hands and knees and turned around, giving Alex and the camera a full view of my ass in its tiny tight green bottom. I straddled the sand, and bounced my ass towards the camera and the photographer.

"Hold on," Alex said. I froze, worried that maybe I'd gone too far.

Instead, he returned with a large bottle of water. He slowly started pouring the cool liquid on my ass, making the fabric see-through and even clingier to my curves. "That's better," he said.

He went back to his camera and took some pictures of my slippery ass while stroking his cock over his pants.

I flipped over onto my back on the fake sand and reached into my bikini bottoms, finally stroking my throbbing pussy. I moaned, and closed my eyes to the "click click" of the camera. I rubbed my clit harder and faster until I couldn't take it any more and I finally came, pulsating my juices onto the already-soaked swimsuit.

"That was a moment to capture," Alex said, his erection fully visible in his khakis.

I sat up in the sand. "Care to make another? Set that camera to auto and come here," I said.

Alex did as he was told: he set the camera to an auto timer and joined me on the faux-beach. He licked my nipples and pulled at the strings of my bikini until I was naked in the sand.

I unzipped his pants and released his huge erection. Grasping it with both hands, I bent down and licked the tip of his massive cock. Alex leaned back. "Turn a bit this way," he said. I realized he was still concerned with the camera, and so I let him move and adjust my position as I stroked and sucked his cock.

"Mmm, that's better." Alex said, pushing my head down deeper onto his cock. He let me blow him for a few minutes, and then he flipped me onto my stomach. He fingered my pussy from behind with one hand, while he slapped my ass with the other. "What a sexy mark that makes," he murmured, pulling my hips up to showcase it to the camera, which continued to click on its own every few moments.

With my ass firmly in his face, Alex began to lick the rim of my asshole. I shivered. No one had ever gone anywhere near it before, and it was tantalizing. Slowly, he pushed one of his fingers into my ass and moved it in slow rhythmic circles. I moaned and winced a bit as he adding another finger and then another—soon he was finger fucking my ass with three fingers, and I couldn't help but buck against him.

Then, in a flash, I felt the thick tip of Alex's cock pushing at the rim of my asshole. I screamed with pleasure as he shoved it in. "Take it," he ordered, and I obliged. At first, I thought Alex's monster cock might split me open, but the pain felt so good I didn't tell him to stop. He spat on my ass to give it more lubricant, and started pushing deeper and deeper inside me.

"Fuck, you're so tight," he moaned. I grabbed my tits, pinching my own nipples hard, wanting to capitalize on the new and delicious pain. Alex fucked me faster, thrusting inside me and slapping my ass. Then, when I thought I couldn't take it for a second more, he pulled out and shoved his cock into my dripping wet pussy.

The shock of the change made me cum violently, screaming and convulsing. I hadn't cum in so long, I almost forgot how good it felt.

"Aw, where do you want me to come?" Alex groaned as he thrust hard into my pulsating pussy.

"Wherever it would look best on

camera," I gasped. My words set him off, and he came hard inside me, filling my pussy with load after load of hot cum.

"Fuck, you said you were out of practice?" He said, gasping for breath as he rolled out of me and onto his back, his dick still dripping with cum. Within moments, I could feel his cum leaking out of me and onto the sand.

"I never modeled like this before," I laughed. "Speaking of which, I'm not sure how well the magazine will like these...... do we have another swimsuit? This one's pretty much drenched in sex?"

Alex laughed and looked around the studio. "Don't worry," he said. "This isn't my first time on set." He slapped my ass and handed me a bag marked "Backup wardrobe for shoot."

Twenty minutes later, I had changed into the spare suit, a sexy black one-piece maillot and was posing like a nice mommy on the beach. The assistants and production people began streaming back in from lunch and bustling around.

"Wow," the bossy swimsuit lady said, looking over Alex's shoulder at the images. He had put most of our earlier shoot onto a separate hard drive that he promised he would make a copy of and send to me later as a private souvenir of my return to modeling. "She looks great, where'd she get that glow? Nice work."

I grinned as the makeup artist came to touch me up. "You really do look great. I think it must have been the bronzer I used on your cheeks." I shrugged and she dropped her powder brush.

"Sorry!" I said.

The makeup artist laughed. "Don't be silly. You really have been out of this game for a while, eh? Most of the models I work with aren't this sweet."

"Hey," she said, feeling around the sand with her hand, looking for the dropped brush. "Why is this sand so wet and sticky?"

Alex just winked at me trying to suppress a laugh.

7 BOWLING BALLS

Sometimes, you just have to relax and go with the flow; however, following a stress-free lifestyle can be tricky when you're knee-deep in your senior year of college.

For the last four years, I've been totally focused on my studies — I've been so engrossed with going to class and studying, that I haven't had time to make or maintain any friendships. Also, I've been so busy that look like shit. My long, golden-brown hair is frizzy, my once luscious curves are dwindling, and I'm pale from spending so many hours inside sitting at the computer.

"Maria, you've got to make a change," my mom told me over the phone a few days ago. "I'm so proud of you and how hard you work, but I'm worried about you. Please promise me that you'll make an effort to go out, have some fun and meet some people?

I sighed. "I appreciate your concern mom, but I just don't want to lose focus."

"Why don't you join a study group then?"

"Ok, I'll think about it," I said. "Bye mom, I love you."

"Love you too, honey," mom said.

The next day, I was studying in the library when I felt a tap on my shoulder. I looked up, eyes tired, to find a strikingly hot guy smiling down at me.

"Hey there," he said. "I noticed that you're reading the textbook for Professor Smith's 4th-year geology... I'm in that class too. I was wondering if you wanted to join our study group?"

I've never joined a study group before because I find it easier to focus alone, but my mom's request for me to be more social was still in my mind. Also, this guy was insanely sexy: he was tall and lean with rich, chocolate brown eyes and an adorable smile.

"Sounds cool," I said. "When and

where?"

"Tomorrow night. Why don't you give me your number and then I'll text you the details," the guy said.

I wrote down my number on a piece of notebook paper and handed it to him with a smile. His fingers lingered on my hand as I gave him the paper.

"I'm Steve," he said.

"It's nice to meet you," I said. "I'm Maria.

A few days later, I had plans to meet up with Steve and the study group for a study session and bowling night.

While I would normally spend my day doing homework, I found myself unusually excited. I tried on all my outfits, and finally settled on a casually sexy pair of skinny jeans and a slightly see-through black blouse. I put on makeup and did my hair for the first time in months, and stopped to admire my work. I looked good.

As I looked at my polished image in the mirror, I couldn't help but think of Steve. I thought about his smile. I thought about his style. I thought about how big his cock might be under his tight pants.

The more I thought about him, the wetter I could feel my pussy getting under my clothes. I lightly touched my breasts, feeling the silky smoothness of the fabric of my blouse. Mesmerized, I decided to take off my clothes and explore my body a bit more.

I left my clothes in a pile on my dorm room floor and lay on the bed. I let my hands graze my skin before finally settling on my clit. I slowly circled the crest of my clit, spreading my juices over myself. I stuck a finger into my pussy and swirled it around, feeling the nerves inside myself tingle.

I was really getting into stroking myself off when suddenly there was a knock at the door. I froze, and realized that I had left my room unlocked. The handle started to turn, and I threw a blanket over my naked body.

"Hey," Steve said, walking into my room. "I thought that maybe you'd like to walk to study group together..." He took a look at the pile of clothes on the floor, then at me — I was naked with nothing but a thin blanket covering me, I was blushing beet red with embarrassment, and my fingers were dripping wet with pussy juices.

"Were you, uh, taking a nap?" he said, grinning mischievously.

"Um. Yes. I was napping. But I'd love

to go with you. Give me a minute to get changed?"

"Sure," Steve said. "Why don't I help you?"

Steve closed the door behind him and walked over to my pile of discarded clothes on the floor. He picked up my bra and reached for my hand. I stood up and let the blanket fall to the floor. Steve stood inches away from me and gently kissed each of my nipples, cupping my tits in his large hands. Then, confusingly, he put my bra on.

I looked at him, confused.

"I said I'd help you get dressed," he said. "We do have to go to that study group."

Then, he picked up my thong from the floor. He crouched down and licked my clit, digging his tongue deep into my crack. After a moment, he held out my thong and I stepped into the leg holes. With a final kiss to my drenched pussy, he pulled them up. Next, he stroked my leg as he helped me into my jeans. Then he kissed and licked my belly before putting on and buttoning up my blouse.

When I was dressed — and thoroughly wet and bothered — Steve grabbed my hand.

"Okay, you look great! Let's go," he said.

It was hard to keep my mind on the books at the study group after Steve and my encounter in my room. He sat beside me and, as the others quizzed the group on geology, Steve stroked my pussy over my jeans. I squirmed in my seat and tried to focus, but after about an hour of the teasing, I started to worry that the wetness in my panties would seep through my jeans and I grabbed his hand under the table.

At first, Steve seemed a bit put off my removal of his hand — until I reached for his crotch. Even through the thick fabric of Steve's tight skinny jeans, I could feel how hard his dick was. I pet him, gently at first, then harder, gripping the outline of his cock like it was dinner and I was starving.

Finally, the oblivious group decided that we had studied enough, and everyone got up to move to our next location: the bowling alley.

The bowling alley was only a 10-minute walk from the library, but it was the longest 10 minutes of my life. A group of guys surrounded Steve as soon as we started walking, so I followed the group awkwardly by myself.

Inside, we all got shoes and paid for a game. While everyone was putting on their shoes and entering names into the scorekeeper, I couldn't stand it any longer — I needed to get off. I excused myself and went to the bathroom.

In the ladies room, I locked myself in a stall and quietly unzipped my pants. I reached in and found my clit and started rubbing it frantically — I didn't want anyone to notice that I was gone. Luckily, I was already super turned on.

I was just about to come, when there was a quiet knock on the stall door. I froze, but then I saw a pair of familiar sneakers peaking under the door. It was Steve.

I opened the stall and Steve was all over me in an instant. He burrowed his face into my breasts, then moved down to my exposed pussy. He bit at my clit, sucking hard. Finally, I felt my pussy surge and convulse as I came.

"There," Steve said. "Now, it's my turn."

He unzipped his pants and pulled out his already hard cock. I sat on the toilet so that my mouth was level with his dick, and I grabbed it. I spat on his dick, and rubbed it all over him so that he was thoroughly lubricated — then I stroked his dick hard.

"Suck it," he said, grabbing my hair and pulling my face towards him. I looked up at Steve and started licking his cock.

"Don't just lick it," he said. "Suck it, please."

I obliged, sucking hard. I sucked as hard as I could, until the tip of his cock struck the back of my throat. I tried hard not to gag, but Steve kept pushing my head further and further down his shaft.

Suddenly, we heard the bathroom door swing open — we froze.

"Uh, Maria? Are you in here? It's your turn," a girl's voice called.

I pulled my face off of Steve's cock and coughed. "Yup! Out in a second!" I called.

"Ok," the girl said. I heard the door slam behind her.

"So," Steve said. "Let's play one game. Then, meet me out back?" He smiled.

"See you there," I said. I kissed him and unlocked the stall door.

Bowling with your study group is hard when you're incredibly turned on. Every time Steve took his turn, I couldn't help but notice the bulge in his pants, and how much I wanted to grab his ass. Distracted, I bowled like shit until the game was — thankfully — finally over.

"Another round?" a girl from the study group eagerly started to put all of our names in for another game.

"Uh, you know what? I think I'm just going to call it a night," I said, while making eye contact with Steve.

"Are you sure, Maria? I think you might need some extra practice. You came in dead last," the girl said, condescendingly.

I returned her smug little smile. "Yup, I'm sure. Bowling might not be my forte. I'm good at other things though," I said sweetly as I pulled off my ugly rented bowling shoes.

I waited for about 10 minutes outside the bowling alley, and there was no sign of Steve. Feeling foolish and rejected, I started walking through the parking lot to the street.

Suddenly, I felt a hand grab my shoulder from behind. I whirled around, afraid to face a mugger. Luckily, it was Steve.

Before I could say a word, Steve pressed his lips against my lips with a passionate kiss. I moved my tongue into his mouth and grabbed his crotch. Steve moved his hands under my blouse and groped my tits; I was instantly wet.

Steve pressed me against the hood of the closest car, and climbed on top of me. I unzipped his pants and pulled out his dick. I started to stroke it, but he pulled my hand away. "I want to be inside of you," he whispered in my ear.

I unbuttoned my pants and wiggled out of them. "Fuck me," I said.

Steve shoved his dick inside me. For a moment, we lay together, enjoying the feeling of Steve's cock stretching my pussy. Then, Steve slowly moved it out and thrust himself in and out of me. I spread my legs as wide as possible as Steve moved on top of me. He started fucking me harder and harder, until I could feel the car shake beneath me, and it felt like the hood was going to cave in.

"What the fuck? Get off my car!" an old man walked up to us.

"Shit, sorry," Steve said. He pulled out of me, grabbed our pants, and grabbed my hand. "Let's go Maria!"

We ran as fast as we could, much to the old man's chagrin, until we reached the nearby forest.

"That was close," I said, covering my

naked pussy self consciously. "Maybe we should just call it a night."

"Sure," Steve said. "I just want to finish one thing."

He pushed me up against a tree and shoved his cock into me from behind. He bucked hard against me, until he screamed, filling my pussy with load after load of his hot cum. He pulled out of me, letting the cum trickle down my leg.

I turned around and smiled at Steve.

"Good study group," I said. "I feel like I learned a lot."

"Same time next week?" Steve said.

"You're on."

8 HYDRATION

Sometimes, it's just easier when you're wet.

Working at the Strawberry County Public Pool for five years now, I'd seen it all: kids putting (often disgusting) things into the water, seniors crawling across the pool slower than a snail, and girls losing their tops in the pool filter. Through it all, I'd been there to help out, always ready to strip down to my red one-piece and dive in.

But, lately, things have become frustrating at the pool. New management took over and started filling the pool with ridiculous bureaucracy. With every day being a drag, I was ready to either quit or explode.

"Ash, you okay?" my friend and fellow

lifeguard, Blake, said to me as I stood at the edge of the pool filling out paper work with a scowl on my face.

"Yeah, thanks," I said. "Just sick of all this paper work. It really takes the fun out of the pool."

"I hear you. What do you say you and me stay a bit late and break a few rules tonight?"

I looked up from my clipboard, intrigued. Blake had been at the pool for as long as I had, but had been in a long-term relationship ever since we met. I'd always found him attractive, but had filed him in my mental "unavailable" bank.

"Isn't Liz waiting for you at home?" I said, cautiously.

"Naw, Liz and I broke up last week. I'm definitely ready to have a bit of fun," Blake said.

I smiled at him. Blake was hot. A former competitive swimmer, he had the rippling body that begged to be in cologne ads. Since he worked at an outdoor pool on the weekends, he also had a killer tan. My decision was clear.

"All right Blake, I'm in," I said. "What did you have in mind?"

"Well... why don't we finish closing things up, then go for a little swim together?"

"Sounds good," I said.

I rushed through the rest of the closing duties as fast as I could. While stacking kickboards, I couldn't help but fantasize about touching Blake's hard, slippery body in the pool. I felt my pussy get wet and blushed.

"Hey, Blake," I called out. "My suit's grungy from teaching lessons earlier. I think I'm going to change into my spare before our swim. You okay to finish up?"

He smiled at me. "Of course, babe."

I ran back into the staff change room and assessed the swimsuits I had to choose from. Most of my suits were fairly conservative for work, but in the back, I found a sexy black halter-top bikini. I grabbed it and pulled off my work suit. I caught my reflection in the mirror and stopped to assess my body. It looked good: I did, after all, spend my whole day swimming and chasing after kids. I moved my hands over my small, supple breasts, down my waist and over my pussy. I rubbed it, releasing my juices and sighed.

Getting an idea, I reached back into my locker and grabbed my razor — I wanted to be competition-smooth for Blake. I stepped into the staff shower and lathered my pussy with shaving cream. I ran the blade delicately over the lips of my vagina, being careful not to knick myself. The gentle caress sent tingles from my crotch to my tits. I rinsed off, squirming with desire, and slipped into the black bikini. Ready.

"Wow," Blake said, as I walked onto the pool deck. He had finished work and was lounging, shirtless, at the side of the pool. I strutted towards him. He reached for me, and I walked past him and dove into the pool.

Blake and I swam in circles, getting closer and closer as our drenched limbs grazed against each other. I teased him like this for a few moments until he couldn't take it any longer, and he grabbed me.

We tred water, our legs beating below us as he held me in the cool water. Then, he kissed me. It was more passionate than I was expecting, as he shoved his tongue eagerly down my throat. The sensation of being dominated overcame me, and we sank into the pool, swirling our tongues as we swirled our legs.

When it became too much, we burst

up for air. I was about to kiss him again, but Blake took off, stroking quickly towards the shallow end of the pool. I followed, my heart racing from the sudden sprint and from the anticipation.

As I reached him, Blake launched at me, running his hands over my tits. I reached into his swim trunks and founds that — even in the cool water — his cock was huge and hard. I held my breath and bobbed my head under the water to make a seal with my mouth on his cock. Over and over, I dove my head under and pulled up on Blake's dick until I ran out of all my breath and had to come up, gasping for air.

Blake untied my top and threw it onto the pool deck.

"It's my turn," he said, and I leaned against the edge of the pool as Blake dove his head under. He pulled off my bikini bottom so that I was completely naked and vulnerable in the water, then he licked my pussy. He came up for air and kissed me, as he shoved his fingers deep into my pussy. I moaned. He fingered me hard until I was just about to come, then he pulled me out of the pool.

"You're so fucking hot, I've got a great idea," Blake said, grabbing my hand. We ran across the pool deck, and I couldn't help but get more turned on as we were at work but totally naked.

Blake took me to the hot tub that he had just cleaned and shut down. Normally, the procedure for starting up the hot tub at work took about 15 minutes, but Blake proved that the new rules were inefficient — he pressed a few buttons to start it up, and the hot tub burst to life with jets.

He kissed me, grabbing my ass in two handfuls. I pressed my hips against his cock, which seemed to have grown even bigger and harder in our journey.

"I'm really glad you're single now," I said, licking my lips as I stroked him.

"Me too. I've been watching your tight ass for years," Blake said.

I turned around, and rubbed my naked ass cheeks teasingly against his cock. Blake admired my show for a moment, then slapped my ass hard.

"You better get in the tub, Ash," he said. He slapped me again and I climbed in, and the steamy heat stung my skin in a delicious mix with my cool insides. Blake eased himself in next to me and immediately started kissing and groping me. Then, he picked me up and leaned me over so that one of the powerful hot tub jets was aimed at my pussy.

"Oh, fuck," I moaned. Blake held me floating in the tub, and teased me by pushing me closer and farther from the jets. Finally, the pressure was so intense that I felt like I was going to explode. "Please, fuck me now," I screamed.

Blake grinned mischievously at me. "Oh, I'm going to fuck you on every surface of this place. But first I want you to fuck this jet until you come." He pushed me closer to the base of the jet. I clung to him, and he bounced me hard against it, my ass slapping the cool tile. The tension built inside me until I finally came, screaming as my juices mixed into the steamy swirling pool.

"There, that's better," Blake said. "Now, what do you say we take a little sauna?"

Panting with pleasure, I couldn't only nod and smile.

We entered the sauna, and I was overwhelmed with the steam. I knelt down to lick Blake's dick, but he stopped me.

"I need to be in your pussy. Now," he said. "Lay down."

I did as I was told and lay my body

down on the warm wood bench. The smell of steam and wood was intoxicating. Blake climbed over top of me and pushed my legs behind my head. He reached down and gave my throbbing pussy a lick for good measure, then thrust himself into me. For a moment, he held himself deep inside me without moving, and I just enjoyed the feeling of being stuffed by the sexy man. Then, he pushed himself even deeper inside me and I yelped as my pussy stretched farther than it ever had before.

Satisfied with the feeling, Blake began to fuck me wildly. He thrust in and out of me rapidly, twisting my legs in different directions to change the angle for him.

"Oh yeah, I love your tight pussy Ash!" He screamed. He grabbed both of my ankles and held them high into the air, lifting my ass straight off the bench and fucked me like I was a rag doll. "Fuck, I think I'm going to come," he grunted.

"No!" I yelled. I wasn't finished with him, and I wanted more. I pushed him away. "Not yet. Lick my tits."

Blake looked at me for a moment — I don't think he was used to a woman telling him how to fuck, and I worried that maybe I'd gone too far. But then, he leaned over me and began licking and sucking on my erect nipples. He reached down to stroke himself, but I grabbed his wrists. "Not yet," I said. He bit down on my nipples, which by now were covered in thick beads of sweat from the heat. "Ok," I moaned. "Now."

Blake flipped me over and I waited eagerly on my hands and knees for his cock. Paying me back for teasing him before, he pushed just the tip into my pussy. I tried to buck against him, but he firmly grabbed my hips so that he was in control.

"Please?" I said, seductively. My plea worked, and Blake started fucking me, piercing me with his dick. He grabbed my long hair and twisted it into a long rope, which he used as a handle as he leaned back. We worked ourselves into a rhythm, and the farther he leaned back, the closer the tip of his cock got to my G-spot. Finally, he leaned far enough and the sensation of my hair being pulled and the head of his dick rubbing my spot were enough, and I came again, the walls of my insides contracting and squeezing hard on him.

"Ah, oh my god!" He screamed, bucking wildly against me until he couldn't take it any longer. He pulled out and came on the small of my back and my ass cheeks. I waited, coming down myself, as he spasmed and emptied his balls onto my body.

"Mmm," I said, moaning in pleasure.

"Yeah," Blake said with a laugh. "I wonder what the correct procedure is for cleaning up this in the pool?"

We collapsed on each other, giggling in a heap of sweat and sex in the sauna.

To cool off, we decided to jump back in the cool pool. Under water, I let Blake run his hands over my body, cleaning the drops of cum off of me and massaging my body. I ran my hands over Blake's washboard abs. When we were clean, we climbed out of the pool, totally satisfied.

We collected our swimsuits, turned off the lights, and walked back into the staff change room to grab our things. As we walked in, we were startled to see our boss, Joshua, standing there, arms crossed.

"Have a good swim, guys?" He asked.

Blake and I looked at each other nervously. Blake then broke into a smile.

"Hey Josh... why don't Ash and I show you some of the new procedures we've developed tonight?" Blake took off his shirt, untied my bikini top, grabbed both of our hands, and walked us out to the pool deck.

I sighed, realizing — as Joshua tentatively grabbed my ass — for the first time that sometimes breaking the rules can be more exhausting than just following them.

9 SWEDISH DESIGN

Working as an interior designer, 'Style' is my middle name. So, when my best friend, Sally, begged me to take on her brother, as a client, I was a bit worried. Sally's brother, Randy, isn't exactly flush with cash, so I knew I wouldn't be able to go to my usual high-end boutiques and order the best of the best online. Still, I loved Sally, and Randy, apparently, really needed the help, so I took on the case.

According to Sally, Randy wanted to redo his apartment, to help bolster his love life. As a fledgling graphic designer, Randy worked from home and had a hard time meeting women. Whenever he did meet a girl, she was less than impressed with his college-style bachelor pad.

"So, does he have any money?" I asked Sally, over coffee, at a local café, as we waited for Randy. Since Randy and I had never met, Sally thought it would be a good idea to introduce us and let us loose, to browse some stores.

"Well, he's got a bit. But, he's still starting out, so not tons. I really appreciate you helping him out, Lindsey," Sally said. "I worry about him being alone, and I think this will make a big difference. You can work miracles!"

I sighed. I could work miracles with cashmere and designer paint. I wasn't sure this would be worth it, even for Sally. I looked at my watch. "Where is he? My time is money, Linds..."

"There he is!" Sally said, jumping up, from her seat, and smiling. I took a sip of my coffee, while Sally smothered the man, who had just entered, with hugs.

"Lindsey, this is my brother, Randy," she said.

I looked up, with my most professional facial expression, and extended my hand. "Hi there, I'm..." I trailed off. Randy was gorgeous. He was tall and tanned, with lush, dark hair and chocolate brown eyes. Dressed casually, in black pants, a T-shirt, and a zip-up hoodie. He was clearly a diamond in the rough. Randy shook my hand, and I felt a tingle run through my body. I wasn't going to make my biggest commission that day, but I had a good feeling about where this was going.

We left Lindsey and I took Randy to the best place I could think of, a big-box store that sold poor-quality, but cheap and trendy furniture, and home decor. We went to the top floor, which was full of showrooms with sample layouts, featuring the store's products.

"So..." I said, taking Randy's arm as we browsed. "I know what Lindsey's told me, but what are you looking for?"

He laughed. "On what? An apartment? Or a woman? I know why my sister wants me to redecorate. She thinks it'll get me laid"

"Well, maybe it will," I said. Randy blushed and put his hands in his pockets.

"Ok, well, don't worry. I have incredible taste, and I can totally help you get laid," I said. I led him into a sleek, masculine bedroom set up. I sat on the plump bed and leaned back provocatively, crossing my legs under my sleek, black pencil skirt.

Randy walked around the room, opening drawers in the dresser, looking around. Then, he hopped onto the bed, beside me. He lay down on his back and turned to look at me. "This is pretty nice," he said.

I lie down, as well, and let my hand rest on his hip. "Yup, I think this sort of look could definitely work for your bedroom," I said, moving my hand slowly from his hip towards his crotch. "It's turning me on, that's for sure."

I let my hand reach his crotch, and found a hard tent. I was about to straddle him, when I heard the giggles of teen girls walking by the display. We stood up.

"Let's keep looking," I said, grabbing Randy's hand. We looked through a few more bedroom sets, all of which were full of shoppers. Then, I found a living room set up and I pulled Randy in.

"I don't know about this one," he said.

"Yeah, it's pretty ugly," I said. "I bet there won't be many people wanting to check this one out." I pushed Randy up against the wall, which was decorated with garish printed wallpaper, and kissed him. He stood still for a moment, surprised. Then, he grabbed me and turned around. So, my back was pressed against the wall. He grabbed my ass and lifted me. I wrapped my legs around his back. We made out, and I could feel his cock getting harder and harder.

He put me down and I stood up. We moved to a black couch, in the display, that was out of sight of the store's aisles. I could feel my pussy aching. I let Randy unzip my shirt and take off my blouse. Stripped of my clothes, I took off his shirt and climbed on top of him, in nothing but my delicate mesh-lace panties, which were decorated with tiny flowers. As much as I disliked the decor of the room, I thought that my slim, sexy body in my luxury panties probably made it look a lot better.

I undid Randy's pants, and released his cock.

"Lindsey," he panted, "this is pretty hot, but what if we get caught?"

"Don't worry," I said. "I wouldn't be caught dead here, professionally, under normal circumstances. Now, let's test out if some new furniture could get you laid."

I leaned down and licked his cock. As hard as it was, already, it seemed to grow with each stroke of my tongue. Randy leaned back and groaned. I licked the tip and stroked the shaft with my hand.

After a while, Randy couldn't take it any longer. He pulled me up to him so that we were chest to chest. He slipped the crotch of my panties to the side and slipped his cock into my warm, wet pussy. For a minute, he just held me there, with his dick stuffing my insides, reveling in how good it felt. Then, he started bucking, so that I bounced up and down on him. Keeping his cock inside me, I sat up, so I was straddling him, and started to ride Randy. He felt amazing inside me, stretching my pussy and stroking my insides. I arched my back and rode him harder, reaching down to rub my clit.

Randy closed his eyes, "I'm sorry, but this feels so good, and I haven't been fucked in a while, I'm going to come," he said.

I stopped moving. "Not yet!" I hopped off of him and threw on my clothes.

"No! Seriously? I'm so close!" he said, lying naked, on the couch. I could see that his cock was literally throbbing, but I wasn't ready to finish, yet.

"Deal with it. Come with me," I said.

We walked through more showrooms while holding hands, grabbing a cart along the way. We got a few looks from other shoppers. I guess we did look pretty disheveled, and Randy's erection was fairly obvious.

We stopped at a few places, filling a cart with some decorative items: pillows; photo frames, and other decor. Every time we stopped, I found a way to subtly grope him.

In the kitchen setting, Randy pretended to drop a napkin, and squatted to the ground to pick it up. Instead of just standing, though, his head found its way under my skirt. Since I hadn't bothered to put my panties back on, he had open access to my wet pussy and he took full advantage. While I leaned on a granite kitchen countertop, Randy licked my clit, under my skirt. He bit at the hood of my clit, making me wince with pleasure and pain. Then, he stuck three of his fingers into my pussy. The feeling was so intense I had to grab at the edge of the counter.

"Is everything ok? Anything I can help you find?" One of the store workers said, as he approached me with a friendly smile.

"No," I said through gritted teeth. "I'm just... browsing."

"Are you sure?" the worker said. "You look concerned. Have you heard about our special cabinet pricing?"

"Um," I said, as Randy inserted a finger into my ass. "No."

"Great!" the worker started rambling to me about cabinet prices, not knowing that I was being roughly penetrated in both of my openly wet holes, while he spoke to me. I felt my juices dripping onto Randy's face, under my skirt, and I got wetter and wetter. I was so close to cumming that I started to shake uncontrollably.

"Wow, I can see that you're really excited about these prices!" the worker said. "Let me grab you some more information!"

"Ohhhh! God yes!" I cried as, I finally exploded with a massive orgasm.

"Great!" the worker scurried off. Probably dreaming of his commission, from what he thought was a sale. Randy emerged from under my skirt, wiped his face with the napkin, and we walked off together.

We kept moving through the store, and as we were walking through some bathroom showrooms, Randy grabbed me and pushed me into a standing shower stall demo. The stall was small, made of white porcelain, with a frosted glass door.

"Did you want to do some bathroom

remodeling, too?" I teased.

"I can't wait another minute," he said. "I need to fuck you, now." Randy practically tore off our clothes. Then, he turned me around and started fucking me from behind. I reached my arms above my head and pressed them into the wall of the shower.

I was getting into it, when, suddenly, Randy froze. Another couple had walked into the showroom and we're looking around. We could see their outlines and hear them talking through the frosted glass door of the shower stall.

"I don't know, babe. Maybe, we should wait until we have the baby before we redo the bathroom?" The woman said.

"Yeah, but I'd really like to have it all taken care of, so we don't have to worry. Our shower is shit." The man said.

Apparently, having the couple inches away from us turned Randy on more, as he started to slowly and quietly fuck me, again. I pursed my hips, trying to stay quiet, as Randy's huge cock filled me to the brim.

The couple nattered on, debating the look of the sink and vanity in the display, while Randy thrust harder inside me. He reached around me and groped my tits, pinching the nipples and massaging them roughly. He bit the back of my neck, gently, and pumped me.

Then, with a final thrust, he came hard, inside me.

"Fuck," he groaned, unable to contain himself.

"What was that?" the couple said. The door to the shower burst open, and we were exposed, naked and dripping cum, in the stall.

We dressed as quickly as possible and ran out, past the bewildered couple, out of the store, abandoning our cart. We went to Randy's car and sat inside, bursting with laughter.

"I'm sorry, Randy," I said.

"For what?" He kissed me.

"We didn't get anything for your apartment. I didn't do my job, and I take my job very seriously," I said.

He laughed. "Are you kidding me? I wanted to redo my place to get me laid... I'd say you did your job better than I ever could have imagined. But, I was wondering..." He reached over and stroked my thigh. "Do you, maybe, want to still come over and take a look at how my place is, now? Maybe, you could do a bit more... consultation?"

10 FINE FURNISHING
Swedish Design Part 2

Sometimes, things just come together in the most unusual ways — and they simply fit. That's how I felt yesterday, when I spent the day assembling cheap furniture with my new client, Randy.

As an upscale interior designer, I don't usually assemble anything. In fact, as a rule, I never buy anything for clients that doesn't arrive put together. But I took on Randy as a favor for my friend Sally. Randy is her brother, and he's broke — he was looking to redecorate to meet girls. And, well, he met me.

Last weekend, I met Randy for the first time and our chemistry was unbelievable. We went to a big, cheap furniture store and I was really surprised by how cute some of the cheap furnishings were. I was also pleasantly surprised by how cute Randy was, and by how well he fucked me in every corner of the store.

While we didn't have time to buy anything during our trip, I went back during the week and picked out some key pieces (I am a professional, after all). I arrived at Randy's apartment with a truckload of boxes and pieces, and he was just as sexy as I remembered. Randy opened the door for me, dressed in a suit and tie.

"Well, don't you look slick," I said. He grabbed the boxes I was carrying from my hands.

"Thanks Lindsey," he said. "I'll change in a second. I just came from church."

I shut the door behind me. Randy was hot the last time I'd seen him, but he'd been dressed in the scrubby casual clothes of a guy without an office. Now, his once-unruly dark black hair was slicked to the side, and his lean build was framed by the crispness of his suit and white shirt. Although I knew that the truck outside was full of boxes, I couldn't help but be turned on by this new, faithful man.

"Hold on a second. I think we can start by unpacking a few things already in here," I said. I pushed him down onto the only chair in the near-empty room. "Let me start."

I began to strip. I had dressed casually for the manual labor, but still sexy in fitted, tight jeans and a black ruffled T-shirt. I unbuttoned my jeans and stepped out of them, leaving on my black high heels. I pulled my top over my head and threw it onto the floor behind me. Randy let out a low sigh at my surprise: under my casual clothes, I was wearing a sexy see-through black bra, thong, and garter belt.

"Wow," Randy said. "Yeah, let me get to work." He reached for me and ran his finger up my thigh until he reached my pussy. He gently fingered the mesh, and I could feel a rush of wetness in between my legs. He pulled me closer to him, and pulled at my thong with his teeth, burrowing his tongue into the grove of my clit. I moaned, and took a step to the side so that my legs were wide and he had easy access. He moved the cloth covering my mound to the side, and thrust his tongue deep into my clit, licking me in circles that sent shockwaves from my crotch to my toes.

When I was close, he bit at the tip of my clit.

"That feels amazing," I said, pulling at his thick hair.

He moved to stand up; I pushed him back down. "You're not done yet," I said, pulling at his hair again, directing his head into my crotch. I pulled him to me, almost smothering him with my pussy. He moaned and moved again, but I pulled him back. Responding to my aggressiveness, he licked and sucked at my clit until I finally found myself begin to shake. My body grew warmer and I pulled tightly at Randy's hair as I came hard, convulsing and pushing my juices onto his face. Finally I let go of Randy's head, and he leaned back and sucked in air. I knelt down to Randy's level and gently licked the pussy juices off of his face.

Finally satisfied, I climbed onto the chair and leaned back. "Ok," I said. "Now you can get to work."

Randy changed out of his suit and into his casual clothes, and moved the boxes from the truck into his place. I sat, still clad in my sexy black under things, and told Randy where to put them.

An hour later, the apartment was filled with boxes and was an absolute mess.

"So, where do we start?" Randy said.

"Well, you've been working pretty hard. Maybe we should take a break," I said, standing up. "One thing we don't need to put together is your bed..."

Randy took the hint. He picked me up and carried me to the bedroom.

"Throw me on the bed," I said.

"Not yet," Randy said. He kissed me hard and pushed me against the wall. I wrapped my legs around him and let him kiss my neck. Then I reached down and unbuckled and unzipped his jeans; they fell to the floor. I could feel Randy's stiff cock pressing into my crotch. He reached down and pulled his dick out of his boxers and shoving my panties to the side, thrust himself inside me. I moaned as Randy fucked me hard against the wall, bouncing me up and down on his cock as My back rubbed against the wall. I clung my arms around his neck and tried to stay steady, but my weight kept drawing me farther and deeper onto Randy's dick.

He pulled away from the wall and threw me onto the bed. "Now you can go on the bed," he said.

Randy climbed onto the bed beside

me, then crept down. He grabbed the side of my panties with his teeth and pulled them down to my ankles and off, spitting them onto the floor. He left my garter belt and stocking on and knelt down to give my pussy a hearty lick.

I squirmed out from under him and climbed on top. "My turn," I said. Slowly, I used my teeth to undress Randy. I took off his T-shirt, then his socks, then his boxers, so that Randy lay stark naked on the bed. Starting at his toes, I licked at Randy's skin like a cat, carefully avoiding his hard, engorged dick. When I'd licked Randy's entire body, I finally drew back down to his hips and let my tongue graze the head of his cock.

I licked his shaft from bottom to tip, then sucked down — stuffing as much of Randy's dick down my throat as I could. Randy grabbed my long hair and coiled it around his wrist like a harness, pulling my face to the exact positioning that his cock craved. I sucked and slurped as his hands guided my mouth harder and faster until he finally shoved my face down onto him and held it over his throbbing dick. I resisted the urge to choke, and felt the salty taste of Randy's warm cum rinse through my mouth.

After a few minutes, he relaxed and let go of my head. I swallowed his load and lay down beside him.

Suddenly, he jumped up off of the bed — clearly recharged. "Let's get to work!" he said.

A few hours later, Randy and I were having a surprisingly good time assembling cheap furniture together. We were working on putting together Randy's new and funky red coffee table when there was a knock at the door. We were hardly dressed for company — Randy was shirtless and in sweatpants, and I was wearing nothing but one of Randy's button-up shirts.

"I'll get it," Randy said, giving me a kiss as he stood up.

Randy opened the door, and I caught a glimpse of a beautiful blonde woman.

"Hey, I live next door," the woman said. "Do you think you could keep the banging down? Sorry, it's just that I have an exam tomorrow and I need to study."

"Banging...?"

"I assume you're redecorating," she said. "I saw the truck. Just try to keep it down."

Randy laughed. "Oh, yeah. Sorry, we'll try to keep things down." He shut the door and walked back to me. He leaned over me and whispered in my ear "I think the neighbors want us to cool it with all the banging..."

I grinned. "I don't know if we can do that."

"Sure, we can be quiet." Randy lunged at me and I playfully dodged out of his way, accidentally knocking over the half assembled coffee table with a crash and a thud. We erupted in a fit of giggles, and suddenly I felt Randy's cock growing hard.

"Put it in me now," I said. Randy obliged, shoving his hard cock into my pussy, which I was surprised to find was already dripping wet.

Randy began to fuck me on the floor, when suddenly the front door to the apartment burst open and the blonde woman walked in.

"Look, I just told you I need you to be quiet, and now you're banging louder than ever," she said, storming into the room. The woman looked at us — Randy with his dick thrust inside me as we lay on the floor — and her mouth gaped open.

"Oh my goodness," she said. "I'm so sorry. Oh my god." She seemed to be both horrified and excited, and she lingered in the room.

Randy pulled out of me. "Erica, this is my... interior decorator Lindsey. She's really good."

"Oh, hi Lindsey," the neighbor said, looking around the apartment, which was still pretty much in shambles. "The place looks... good."

"Do you want to help us?" Randy said, his naked cock showing his eagerness. "I'm sure Lindsey would agree that we could really use another pair of hands. Maybe it could relax you and help you study?"

Erica walked into the room and knelt down beside us. She was dressed in typical grad school clothes: a ratty sweater and holey jeans. I pulled her sweater over her head, and found that she was totally naked underneath. I cupped her breast and was shocked at how warm she was.

Erica had beautiful teardrop-shaped breasts, and I began slowly licking and kissing them, as Randy took his cue and unbuckled her jeans. He pulled them down and fingered her pussy. Erica moaned — I doubted that she'd had this much attention in a while.

After a while, Erica lay down on her back on the floor. Randy slid inside her, and began slowly pumping her with his dick. I climbed on top of Erica, so that my pussy hovered over her face. She began to tentatively lick me, and I lowered myself further, so that she could dig her tongue into my clit. Randy kept fucking Erica, and reached up to kiss me. Randy fucked Erica more intensely, and the harder he fucked her, the harder she sucked on my clit. The sensation got more and more intense, and I came hard on Erica's face. A moment later, Randy fucked Erica wildly and groaned, filling her pussy with another load of his warm cum.

I sat back, and Randy pulled out. Erica lay frozen and fucked, on the floor. I smiled at her.

"Don't worry girl, I won't leave you hanging," I said. I crawled over her, and spread her legs wide. A trail of Randy's cum was already starting to trickle out of her pussy. I licked it up and slowly traced the lips of her pussy with my tongue. I slipped my index finger into her pussy and gently bit at her clit. Erica moaned and arched her back as she began to shake. Finally, I started sucking her on her clit and her body exploded in a huge orgasm. She shook for a few minutes and then finally relaxed into the floor.

All three of us lay, sweaty and panting, on the floor staring at the ceiling for a few moments. After a while, Erica got up and started to get dressed.

"Well, that was nice, but I better let you guys get back to work," she said, gesturing around the room — which was a mess of boxes and bits and pieces of furniture.

Erica left, and Randy leaned over to kiss me. "Well," he said. "What do you want to put together next? I think there's a chair that might be fun..."

11 LEMON LIME

"Delicious," I said, licking a hefty dollop of sweet-sour buttercream frosting from the tip of the wooden spoon.

"Yes, you are," Tom said, grinning at me. I made a face at him, making my faux disgust at his cliché clear, though I felt myself flush happily in spite of his corny statement.

Lately, I've found myself thinking more and more that Tom was the best thing that had ever happened to me. With his dark curls and T-shirt-inflating structure, he was the loveliest physical specimen I'd ever been in the same room with. Or had inside me.

As the owner and main baker at Cake Queen's Confectionery, I'd spent a long time working alone, but after hiring Tom a few months ago, my productivity had gone way up in the kitchen and in the bedroom. Work was a dream, though it was often hard to concentrate on baking with my sexy assistant strutting around the kitchen.

The bakery was open, but we'd hit the mid-morning lull and while the street outside was bright and lively, we were alone inside.

I stood at the front counter and began frosting a batch of vanilla cupcakes with the buttercream, creating thick peaks of tasty frosting. Tom walked towards me and picked up one of my creations.

"Have another taste," he said. He placed the cupcake an inch from my mouth. I licked the tip of the cake and moaned with pleasure. He pushed it closer into my mouth, forcing me to lick the frosting faster until I bit into the cake, enjoying the explosion of flavor that permeated my synapses.

I looked around the shop. With no one around, I got on my knees and ran my hand over the bulge at the front of Tom's charcoal work pants. I unzipped his fly and pulled out his member, which was thick with desire. Just as I was about to lick the tip, I heard the familiar jingle of the door. I went to stand up, but Tom placed a hand firmly on my head, keeping me in my place.

I knew it was poor customer service, but I could feel my pussy moisten at Tom's brashness. Tentatively, quietly, I licked the tip of his cock.

"What's good today?" I heard the familiar voice of Andrea Bates, one of our regulars.

"Everything's good. You know that," Tom said playfully, not moving his hand from my head as he stood firm behind the counter.

"Hmm. I'm looking for a treat. Me and Gary broke up last night," Andrea said, laughing sadly. "I know, I know: such a girl thing to medicate with cake. But you guys are the best."

Tom's hand massaged my head, sending tingles down my spine. I let my mouth slip over his now rock-hard cock, engulfing it. I moved my mouth slowly but firmly up and down his cock.

"You know, Tom," Andrea said, oblivious to our behind-the-counter activities. "It seems sort of dead in here... maybe you could find a way to cheer me up?"

I felt Tom grow even harder in my mouth at Andrea's proposition.

"Oh, I'm sure a chocolate torte will do the trick," Tom said, pushing hard on my head until I couldn't help but gag on his thick dick.

"What was that?" I froze and looked up to see Andrea leaning over the counter and peering down at me.

"What the fuck is going on here?" Andrea screeched. I could feel my cheeks flush crimson with embarrassment.

"I... I'm so sorry," I said, standing up. "I don't know what got into me. I know this is so unprofessional." I tried to make eye contact with Andrea, but she looked distracted. I followed her gaze to Tom's still hard dick, now exposed.

"That's... okay," Andrea said, shaking her head. "Just don't do it again, or I'll never shop here again."

Tom leaned over the counter and smiled at her, his cock still out and throbbing hard. "Andrea, why don't you let us make it up to you? We've got some delicious stuff coming out of the oven soon. Come back here."

Andrea paused for a moment and looked at each of us; then she stepped behind the counter and dropped her purse on the floor.

"Show me," she said.

Andrea and I walked back to the kitchen. I could hear Tom in the bakery clicking the door locked and flipping the sign on the door to closed. I looked at Andrea, who leaned slightly uncomfortably against the wall. Andrea was dressed conservatively in a navy blue skirt suit and cream-colored, ruffled blouse.

"I've always wondered, Andrea," I said, trying to break the tension, "what do you do?"

"I'm in investments..." Andrea began, but trailed off as Tom walked back into the kitchen, completely naked.

Tom came to me and pulled my shirt over my head. He unhooked my bra letting my heavy breasts spring free. Tom buried his head in my chest and moaned. For a moment, I forgot about Andrea and ran my fingernails down Tom's back—until I heard a gentle sigh from the corner of the room.

Tom gestured to Andrea to come closer. She stepped towards us and Tom slowly started unbuttoning her blazer. He then worked on her blouse as I watched. Despite the twinge of jealousy I felt watching Tom undressing another woman, I couldn't help but feel turned on as my crotch get wetter and wetter. Tom threw Andrea's clothes on the counter, and she stood naked, her nipples erect.

I began to stroke my pussy as Tom sucked on Andrea's nipples. Andrea had huge nipples—pink and puffy. I wanted a turn. I pushed Tom aside and licked Andrea's right nipple, tentatively at first, as I'd never felt another woman's body touch my tongue before. Tom stepped away and I could see him stroking his cock as he watched me lick and suck on Andrea's puffy nipples.

He came up behind me and pulled my pants and red lace panties down to my ankles. While I suckled Andrea, Tom shoved his hard dick into my wet pussy. The harder he pumped into me, the harder I sucked on Andrea.

I found my hand reaching into her waistband for her pussy. I was surprised to feel how wet she was, so I knelt down in front of her, as Tom continued to thrust inside me from behind. I pulled down her bottoms and licked her wet clit. Andrea spread her legs a bit so that my tongue hit the tip of her clit. She moaned.

Suddenly, Tom pulled out of me.

"Suck my cock," he said. I turned around as instructed, but he pushed me away. "Not you, babe. Her."

Tom lay on the floor, and Andrea knelt in front of him. She was shaking. He grabbed her face and jammed it onto his cock, pushing it up and down. She seemed to get into the rhythm, moaning with her mouth stuffed full of cock.

I sat on the floor beside them, rubbing my clit furiously. Tom reached behind him on the counter and grabbed a rolling pin, handing it to me.

"Use it like it's my cock," he gasped.

I did as I was told, licking the cool marble of the pin until it was slippery. Then, I pushed the thick toy into my pussy as I watched Andrea suck my boyfriend's cock. I'd never been more turned on, and soon I was wildly thrusting the thick pin in and out of myself. I screamed as finally I felt myself begin to shake and my muscles tensed.

"Fuck!" I yelled, as my pussy walls clenched and pulsated against the pin. I pulled it out and lay down, spent.

Meanwhile, Tom pushed Andrea off of his cock, which was thick and puffy with veins from so much blowing.

"Eat her cum," Tom said to Andrea. He was clearly getting off on bossing us around, but Andrea seemed to like it. She knelt before me and took a tiny, delicate lick of my pussy. I was still cumming hard, and the delicate touch was almost more than I could bear.

"Harder," Tom said. Andrea obliged, digging her tongue into my clit and lapping up my juices like it was a vanilla cone. Then, Tom was behind her, looking into my eyes as he fucked her.

"Oh yeah! Yes!" Andrea screamed into my pussy. "It's been so fucking long since I've had a cock in me. Fuck me!" Tom bucked harder against her, using her ample ass as a handlebar. The harder he fucked her, the harder she licked my pussy, and soon I was cumming again.

"Fuck, turn around," Tom said. Andrea was so into the fucking she didn't stop. "Now!" He yelled, pulling out of her and twisting her to face him. Tom came on Andrea's face, frosting her face with warm semen.

Andrea sat stunned for a moment. She wiped the cum off of her face with her hand, and spread it over her glistening breasts.

"That was great," she said. "But don't think I'm going to let you get away with this without making me cum first."

Tom and I looked at each other.

"What do you want me to do?" I asked. Andrea lay on her back, spreading her legs wide.

"I want you to make me cum," she said.

"Hmm…" I crawled over to her and kissed and bit her inner thighs. She groaned with appreciation. Tom handed me the thick marble rolling pin, which was still juicy with my cum. "Maybe this will help," he said.

"Thanks."

I spat in Andrea's pussy to get it extra lubricated, and slowly pushed the pin inside her. I jerked it in and out of her, slowly at first and then faster and faster.

Andrea started bucking against the pin, so I began twisting it, rolling it around the edges of her pussy as I thrust it in and out.

"Do you like that? Is it like I have a big thick cock for you?" I said.

"Fuck, I'm so close," she moaned. I shoved the pin as far into Andrea as I could, then I put the other end of the pin in my own pussy, and began rocking back and forth. The pin stretched both of our pussies, and soon we were frantically bucking against each other.

"Yesssss!" Andrea screamed as she came.

"Wait! I'm so close!" I said, closing my eyes to concentrate as I could feel the waves of pleasure rising inside me. Suddenly, I felt Tom biting down hard on my erect nipples and I came hard.

Andrea and I collapsed into each other's arms, as the marble pin fell onto the floor with a clatter. Tom curled up behind me, and soon we all fell asleep on the floor, covered in cum and satisfied.

We awoke hours later by the sound of the door unlocking. It was night, and the cleaning man was coming in to clean up. He turned on all the lights, blinding us for a moment.

"What the fuck?!" The cleaning man said, standing over us. He laughed. "Busy day at the bakery Anna?"

Andrea jumped to her feet and gathered her clothes, embarrassed. As she stood up, she kicked the rolling pin across the floor.

"Thanks for the... dessert, guys," she said to Tom and me, her cheeks crimson with embarrassment as the cleaning man eyed her lecherously. "I've got to go."

Andrea ran out of the bakery, her clothes half on and backwards.

"So, looks like I've got some extra cleaning to do tonight," the cleaning man said, observing the remnants of our afternoon sexcapades.

"I'm so embarrassed," I said. "I can clean it up myself - don't worry about tonight."

"No, no," the cleaning man said. He walked towards me and stroked my naked breast. "I wouldn't mind cleaning up if I get a little something sweet before and after." He stroked his erection over the top of his pants. I looked at Tom.

"Well," Tom said. "We've got some muffins left from this morning. But Anna's got some lemon-lime cream that's just to die for..."

12 HERE COMES THE TROLLEY

Working in a restaurant is a real grind (I should know — I've worked in nearly 10 over the years), but working at the Trolley Factory was by far the worst. The food sucked, the managers were lazy and we had to wear horrible green costumes. But the worst part of working at the Trolley Factory had to navigate with heavy trays of steaming hot and bland pasta around the huge replica San Franciscan trolley car.

Case in point? Last Friday night. There were two big groups of teenagers flinging forks around, making boisterous comments about the size of my large, round ass in my tight Trolley Factory uniform and generally making my life hell.

The only good thing about the shift was that John was working, too. John and I had dated nearly 10 years ago when we were in high school, and when that didn't work out, had been the best of friends ever since. Working with John made things bearable; he was funny, kind, tall, dark and handsome.

"Well, babe, at least we should be in for some good tips tonight," John said when he saw me balancing a stack of dirty plates on my tray in the kitchen. "You know teenagers just love to give great tips."

I laughed, and accidently dropped the pile. The plates crashed to the floor.

"Nice one. Here, let me help you." John walked up behind me and leaned over me to help pick up the pieces. As he reached behind me, I couldn't help but notice the slight bulge of his cock pressing through his polyester work pants and into the curve of my ass. I was surprised to feel a twinge of wetness between my legs.

We finished cleaning up, and I turned to look at John, who just smiled and winked at me.

The rest of the shift, John and I played an unspoken game, seeing how many times we could rub up against each other. At first, it was fairly innocent, with me brushing my breasts against his back as we delivered plates, or with him pressing his hips into my crotch as we walked past each other in the busy kitchen.

"What's up with you two? You're working as slow as a slug!" Our annoying lead manager, Sandra, said at around 7 p.m. Sandra was classically boring and uptight — slightly overweight and middle-aged, she was the epitome of annoying. We usually tried to avoid her and her tirades at all costs.

John winked at me. "It's just one of those days, I guess. Sorry Sandra," he said. I stifled a laugh.

As the night went on, things began to escalate, as John started groping me every chance he got. While I went to pick up a plate of spaghetti from the window, he stood behind me and slyly shoved his index finger into the groove of my ass. I froze, and let him wiggle it for a moment as my panties got more and more wet.

Later, as we cleared and set a table, I managed to grab the bulge in his pants and give his dick a quick stroke; I was pleased to note that it seemed to be getting harder as the night wore on.

We were flirting hot and heavy when Sandra's screechy voice cut through our sexual tension.

"Kara! John! Break up those kids' NOW, or it's coming out of your paychecks!"

Unable to spare the change, we begrudgingly approached the table to teen boys, who were engaged in some sort of food fight.

"Hey, guys. Just so you know, we've got to keep our food on our plates in here, okay?" I said. The boys laughed at me.

"Hey, why don't you follow that rule then... maybe keep your food on the plate instead of putting so much in your mouth," said a tall, gangly-looking boy. "Then maybe you wouldn't have so much in your ass!"

Even though I knew they were just kids, I couldn't help but blush at the insult. To make matters worse, the kids started flinging their food at each other again — and a long, saucy tendril landed square down the middle of my cleavage.

I blushed and turned to leave, and walked into John's muscular chest.

"Hey!" John yelled. "Just because you're kids doesn't mean you get to be dicks!" A hushed silence filled the room. John turned to me, bent down, and licked the tendril of spaghetti from my chest. The teens' jaws dropped. John grabbed my shoulders. "And the fact that you guys can't appreciate juicy ass like this... just shows that you're all fucking virgins." John grabbed a handful of my ass and slapped it, then he grabbed my arm and we walked away.

"Oh my gosh, John," I said when we were back in the busy kitchen. "I can't believe you did that."

"Yeah, well, it's true," he said, stepping closer to me so that our mouths were only inches apart. He smiled. "Meet me in the trolley in five."

I nodded; my heart beating wildly from the excitement. I grabbed all the food for my tables and rushed it out as fast as I could and, when no one was looking, I slipped into the decorative trolley in the middle of the restaurant.

John was already waiting for me, sitting on the floor of the trolley so that no one could see him. I crawled over to him and opened my mouth to speak — but John shut me up by pulling me on top of him and shoving his tongue down my throat.

Before I knew it, John had burst open my spaghetti-stained uniform top and threw it on the floor. I paused, fully aware of how much trouble we would be in if I got caught, topless, in the middle of the restaurant — but I was so turned on I didn't care. I ripped John's shirt off and pressed my chest against his, rubbing our nipples together as I straddled him.

John grasped my ass. "You do have the sexiest ass I've ever seen. I've been dreaming about it since high school," he said. I turned around on my hands and knees so that my ass was firmly in his face. I looked over my shoulder and grinned at John. "Well, why don't you eat it then?"

John sprung to action, pulling my pants down to my ankles and burying his face in my ass cheeks. He licked me all over, and slapped me so hard I worried that someone would hear. He stuck one finger inside my butt, and another in my dripping wet pussy.

It felt so good, I wanted to scream, but I didn't want to be found out. Sensing my struggle, John used his other hand to grab a white cloth napkin from his pocket and stuff it in my mouth. I bit hard.

John continued to finger both my holes for a while until I was so close to coming, then he pulled out of me. I took the cue and flipped around. With the napkin still in my mouth, I took off John's pants, and started to stroke his stiff cock. Then, I kissed him: transferring the napkin from my mouth to his.

"You're going to need that," I whispered with a wink. I kissed John's neck and moved my mouth down John's chest to his thigh before licking the tip of his dick. John let out a napkin-muffled groan and grabbed my long-blonde hair, pulling it tightly, which only turned me on more.

I teased him, sucking hard at the tip of his cock, before thrusting my whole mouth over his shaft. John started thrusting his hips, fucking my face, while using my hair as handles. While he fucked my face, I pulled down on John's balls, massaging them roughly — making him explode. John groaned into the napkin as he shot his load into my mouth. I swallowed the salty concoction and licked my lips. "Mmm," I said.

John and I leaned up against the side of the trolley car recovering for a moment. Sitting there, the sounds of the restaurant began to fill my ears and I remembered where I was.

"Oh my God," I said "I can't believe we did that in the restaurant. I reached for my shirt. "We better get back out there before anyone notices! Shit — what if that table of teens complains?"

John grabbed my hand to stop me from dressing. "Wait."

"Seriously John, that was great, but we've got to get out there!"

"Babe," John said. "I've waited years for this. And I'm hungry. I'm not leaving this fucking trolley until I'm full."

He threw my shirt back on the ground and pushed me back so that I was laying down. I tried to sit up but he took the napkin and placed it in my mouth, silencing me. He kissed my forehead and got to work.

John dug into my pussy with his tongue — alternating between biting my clit and licking my hole. He swirled his tongue over my clit until I was shaking. He kept licking until I couldn't keep it in any longer: I came hard, spewing my juices into John's mouth. He lapped up my juices.

"Full?" I asked, reaching for my shirt once again, my lower body still shaking from my orgasm.

"Not yet," John said, stroking his again-hard cock.

"Give me more of that ass," he whispered into my ear. I got on my hands and knees and he knelt behind me, mounting me. I bit my lip to stop myself from screaming as John's huge cock stretched my pussy, which was already tight from coming earlier. It felt so good.

"Ride me," I hissed, getting into the motion of John's thrusts. He slapped my ass, hard.

"Where the fuck did John and Kara go?" Sandra's shrill voice cut through the pleasure of our fucking. "Their tables' need their bills!"

We froze. "Should we go?" I whispered to John.

"Fuck no," he said. "We're going to cum, and then we go."

I twisted my back to kiss him. John locked lips with me, sucking hard as he pumped me from behind. I twisted around so that I was straddling him and wrapped my arms around John's back and bounced up and down on his cock. I leaned back in John's arms as he held my ass and used it to slam my pussy up and down on his throbbing cock.

"Awwwww fuck yeah!" John screamed out loud as he shot his hot load inside me. I clasped my hand over his face, but it was too late.

Sandra burst onto the trolley. "What the fuck is going on here? John? Kara?!"

I blushed and John shrugged his shoulders, his cock still inside me.

"We were... taking a break?" I said.

After the restaurant closed, John and I waited nervously for Sandra to dole out our punishment and, most likely, fire us.

We cleaned and closed up, and waited for the other staffers to leave. The other waitresses rolled their eyes at me as they left, while the waiters and cooks gave John high fives and fist bumps. I adjusted my uniform, which was wrinkled and rumpled from our adventures.

Finally, Sandra sauntered up to us.

"So, guys, that was quite a night," she said. "What were you thinking?"

John, always the chivalrous one, tried to take the blame. "Look, Sandra, this is all a big misunderstanding but it was my fault. Some customers were harassing Kara and she needed comforting and one thing led to another... but I know it was unprofessional so if you're going to fire anyone, fire me."

"No," I said. Maybe it was the post-coital bliss, or the fact that I hated my job, but I couldn't let John take it all. "It's my fault."

Sandra raised her hand to us. "Shut it. I don't care why you did it. What I really want to know is if you'd be willing to do it again... and if you'd consider a third."

John and I looked at each other. I shrugged, and he pulled a cloth napkin out from him pocket.

"The trolley awaits, ladies," he said, and we all hopped on board.

13 TOY STORE

Everyone always told me that if I went to college and studied hard and that I would find a good career and have lots of money. Everyone lied.

A year after I finished my business degree, I was struggling to make ends meet working horrible temporary jobs in offices answering phones and making coffee. It was the worst, and it didn't pay shit. If it wasn't for my boyfriend Alex supporting me, I'd be basically homeless.

"Babe, I don't know what I'm going to do," I said, plopping myself down on the couch beside Alex after a long day at work. "I don't know if I can take another day of this. The boss was such a bitch to me today. I want to quit so bad."

Alex rubbed my back comfortingly. "I feel really bad for you, Stacey. You work so hard and all that for nothing. I wish I could be of more help."

"You already do everything! You're the best thing in my life," I said smiling. "Here, let me show you." I flopped onto Alex's lap and undid the zipper on his dark blue jeans. I started stroking his dick to life. He moaned and started lazily running his hand through my hair.

I bit down lightly on his shaft, playfully, and he pulled me up, kissing me softly. I loved Alex, but our sex life was so vanilla. He never wanted to try anything new. I sighed.

Suddenly, there was a knock at the door. Alex pecked me on the cheek and got up to answer it.

"Hey, buddy!" Alex said. It was Alex's friend Jason. I smiled. Jason was one of my favorites among Alex's friends: he was so adventurous, always trying something new.

"Hey guys, I brought wine!" he said. I liked him even more.

A few glasses of wine into the evening, I started feeling very chatty. "The thing is that I think I am pretty smart, just no one will give me a chance to show my stuff," I said. Alex nodded approvingly. "She's right. The market is just so tough for girls like her."

Jason stared at us oddly for a moment. "Do you really feel that way?" he asked.

"Absolutely! I just want to do something with a little bit of excitement!" I proclaimed.

Jason smiled. "Well, Stace, I think I might have some work for you."

"Seriously? Doing what?" I said, intrigued.

"Look, it's getting late—I better go. Here's my card: come by Monday at 8 a.m.," he said. Jason patted Alex on the back and left.

"That's amazing. Jason's always getting in on a new venture," Alex said. "What does the card say?"

I looked down. The card had an address on one side, and a picture of a large, glossy pink dildo on the other.

I showed up at the address on Jason's card at ten to eight on Monday morning. The address was in a warehouse district of town and was a bit hard to find, but Alex and I had mapped it out the night before and I was ready.

Despite the intriguing card, I still wore my typical "work" outfit: a navy skirt suit and a white blouse. Standing at the building's entrance, I caught my reflection in the window. I'd lost a lot of weight recently from the stress of the hunt, and the clothes looked a baggy on my thin frame. Still, I liked how the navy brought out the blue in my eyes, and my hair looked clean and professional tied into a tight bun on top of my head. I smiled at my reflection, and walked in.

Inside, I instantly felt overdressed. The receptionist could have doubled for a stripper—the petite redhead wore a black latex dress that pushed her breasts nearly to her chin.

"Hi there!" the receptionist said warmly. "You must be Stacey! Jason said you'd be coming in. You excited?"

"Er... yes! To be honest, I'm a little bit nervous... I don't really know what this job will involve," I said.

She laughed. "Trust me, you'll love it. Come with me — you've got to change."

The receptionist led me to a back room where a locker was already waiting for me. "Take off all your clothes - you can leave your panties on if you like, but they'll only get in the way - and put it all in here. When you're ready, go through that door and Jason will get you started."

Before I could say anything, she squeezed my ass and was gone, and I stood alone in the room. For a minute, I thought I would leave this crazy place. Did Jason really think of me as a prostitute? Was it porn? I picked up my purse, but then I thought about it a bit. This was, certainly, exciting...

I took off my clothes, neatly folded them, and walked into the workroom.

"Hey, Stace! Welcome to the playhouse!" Jason said as I entered. The "playhouse" was a large warehouse filled to the brim with colorful toys — adult toys. There were tables filled with dildos, vibrators, lubes, creams, plugs, rings, and props of all kinds.

Everyone was naked, and there were several people lounging on couches scattered around the room, playing with the merchandise.

I was awestruck.

"So... you must be wondering about this job," Jason said. "Basically, I've developed a company that provides the most comprehensive quality control testing for adult toys. Upstairs, we develop new products, and then down here, you girls and a few of us guys test things out. It's a great system."

I was leery. "So I just have to masturbate all day?" I questioned.

Jason laughed. "Indeed, I need you to tell me what works and what doesn't. The pay is $200 a day. You in?"

I looked around. As odd as it was, I was pretty turned on. And, maybe more importantly, I was broke. "Maybe I'll just try it out for today..."

"Great!" Jason said. "Today, I'll start you on the Tantric Teddies." He led me to a table of adorable teddy bears. "Here's your response sheet... have fun!"

Jason left and I picked up one of the bears and walked over to a couch. What could be sexy about a teddy bear? I pressed down on its stomach, and suddenly the bear's nose started to vibrate. Oh.

Shy at first, I looked around to see if anyone was watching me — but everyone seemed more interested in their own tasks than in me. I gently ran the shaky nose over my nipples. At first, the vibration was jarring and I had to pull it away. Tentatively, I put it back, letting the bear ignite something inside me. I watched as my nipples grew longer and harder.

Then, I slowly started moving the bear down my body, until his sweet little furry nose was buried in my clit. There was something about the ultra soft, warm fur of the toy caressing my skin while the hard plastic nose stimulated my clit that was too much to handle. I couldn't help but sigh out loud, as my body stiffened and then released into a soothing, relaxing orgasm.

I lay there for a moment as I came down, considering the nature of my new job. Then, I rolled over, picked up the clipboard Jason had handed me earlier and started describing my new experience.

I arrived home from work that afternoon feeling rejuvenated.

"Hey babe!" Alex was waiting for me in the kitchen. "So, what was the job?"

"Well... it was pretty fantastic," I said. "Pays great, too!"

"That's great! So... what is it?"

"I brought some paper work home with me tonight, why don't I show you?"

I grabbed Alex's hand and drew him into the bedroom. I pulled the pins from my bun and let my long brown hair stream down my back. I took off my clothes.

Alex looked confused. "Honey, maybe we should..."

"Shh," I interrupted him. "This is for work." I pulled his T-shirt over his head and unbuttoned his jeans. I grabbed my purse, and pulled out the first of my supplies: a small vibrator in the shape of an egg. "This," I said, "is the EggTeaser 2000. Part of my new job is seeing how fast this can make me cum... and I was hoping that you could help me with my homework."

Alex looked shocked. "Your new job with Jason is testing toys?"

I nodded, and twisted the egg to make it hum. I stroked it lightly over Alex's nipples with one hand. With the other, I reached down and cupped his balls. Alex stiffened, nervous, and I lay down on our bed.

"Watch me, tell me if I'm doing a good job," I explained. He sat down on the edge of the bed, and I began rubbing the egg over my clit. I moved the humming egg in circles from my mound to my clit and back again. Once I started to tingle, I moved the egg lower and lower until it hovered over the entrance to my pussy. I turned the setting so that the egg was at full capacity, and then I shoved it inside my pussy, until it was swallowed so far inside me that it couldn't be seen. I moved my hips up and down on the bed, letting the egg move slightly inside me as I shifted my weight. The tension in my pussy grew and spread through my whole body until I finally burst with pleasure, cumming hard.

I pulled it out of me and switched it off turning to Alex, who sat stunned and erect on the edge of the bed.

"So, how long would you say that took?"

Alex jumped on top of me and ravished me with kisses, groping me with a ferocity that he never had before.

"Wait!" I said. "Grab me my purse."

Alex brought me my purse, and I pulled out a soft ergonomic dildo. "Here, why don't you help me test this?"

Alex grabbed the toy and shoved it into my already soaking wet pussy. "Like that?" he exclaimed.

"Perfect!" I cried out. Alex fucked me with the dildo over and over. When it was soaking wet, he pulled it out and rubbed the tip around the rim of my ass.

Alex thrust his cock into my pussy as he shoved the dildo up my ass. He left the dildo inside, and began pumping me hard.

I panted. "Wait! We have to see how the dildo works in my pussy!"

Alex didn't stop thrusting. "Shhh. This will work."

Alex fucked me harder and harder, and then began to pump the dildo quickly in and out of my ass. The sensation of being penetrated in two places at once was more than I could take, and I came again. I screamed.

Alex groaned and pulled out of my pussy. He came on my face, shooting his load into and around my mouth.

"Ugh," he said, as droplets of his sweat dripped from his chest and onto my mouth, mixing with the already-salty taste of his sperm. "So, do I get a cut of the money for testing that one out?"

The next morning, I walked to work with an extra spring in my step. Today, the redhead receptionist was wearing a sexy leopard-print romper. I handed her a large stack of completed response worksheets.

"Wow!" She said. "You're a natural at this. Jason's going to be pleased."

I winked at her and went to the locker room to strip down.

Back in the workroom, I found Jason and touched his arm.

"Hey! How are you adjusting to the new line of work?" he asked.

"Great! You know, I think I might even be ready for some more advanced work. Maybe some sort of... focus group?"

Jason looked up, surprised. "Cheryl! Lisa!" he called. "Are you guys ready for a team project today?"

14 SMARTPHONE

When I moved to New York to pursue my dream of selling gourmet hot dogs, I was shocked at how impersonal communication was for most people.

I never hated technology, per se, but growing up in a small rural town, I was used to personal communication: if you had something to say, you wrote down their phone number, dialed them up, and spoke with them in real time. Or, better yet, you went to see them and speak with them face-to-face.

Needless to say, it was a big adjustment living in the city that never sleeps, or talks to one another; after a few months, I was feeling pretty lonely. I was pulling pretty long days selling my wiener creations at "Hot Dog!" and wanted to find a way to reach out to my friends back home, so I decided to invest some of my new wiener money in a Smartphone.

So, one night after work, I went to the electronics store: I was shocked and a little afraid of how many options there were and was about to leave when a kind-looking salesman approached me.

"Looking for a new phone?" he asked.

"Yes, well, I've never really had a cell phone, and I work remotely... so I thought that maybe one of these Internet phones could help keep me connected," I said, blushing at how corny it sounded to say it out loud.

"Wow, never had a cell phone before? This is going to be really exciting," he said, placing his hand over mine and smiling reassuringly. "My name's Kyle."

I smiled back at Kyle, who was tall and sandy blonde and looked like he could pass for a professional kitten wrangler if he wanted to. I felt instantly at ease.

Kyle helped me pick out a nice phone, set me up with a plan, and helped me download some apps. "I'm just going to put the essentials on there that I'm sure you'll need. You can check them out and add more when you get home."

"Thanks," I said, taking my bag and

new phone and walking out to leave.

"Oh, and Larissa," Kyle called out after me, "I also programmed my number into your phone—in case you ever want to... communicate."

What a sweet guy, I thought to myself as I left the store and took the subway home.

Once home in my tiny apartment in Brooklyn, I pulled out my new toy. Remembering what Kyle had taught me, I browsed through the programs he'd added: an Internet-browsing function, some games, and a tip calculator. All very useful stuff. Then, a small, bright-orange icon on my phone caught my eye. Tiny letters in the graphic called it "Single & Mingle NY." Intrigued, I touched the button on the screen.

Instantly, the screen was populated with a matrix of provocative photos of super-hot men and women. I panicked and dropped the phone. I picked it up tentatively, and looked at the screen: yes. Still near-naked people. I pressed at the buttons on the phone frantically until the phone reverted to its home screen (with a picture of an adorable puppy).

I couldn't believe Kyle had put that on my phone. I was outraged. I sat and stewed about it for a moment, and then I remembered that I could do something about it. I decided to call him.

"Hey baby, I knew you'd call," a male voice answered.

"Kyle? What kind of sick porno app did you put on my phone," I questioned.

"It's not sick and it's not porno: you said you were lonely and looking to connect," he said. "Try it, and then call me and tell me what you think."

"You're disgusting," I yelled into the phone and, with a bit of technical difficulty, I hung up.

What was he thinking? I was appalled, but couldn't help but take another peek at exactly what it was. Opening the app, I looked more closely at the screen. It read: "Lonely in NY? Set up a sexy profile and our app will help you make the connection you crave."

I scrolled through the app: there were pages upon pages of "profiles" — pictures of people in all states of undress and short descriptions of what they were into. I clicked a few randomly. "Ken" liked guys that were willing to dress up as firemen while they fucked him. "Shawna" wanted guys to eat her out while she licked popsicles.

Confused, I decided to use my phone

for what was meant for, and called my sister Lisa. I told her all about my day, Kyle and the sexy app.

"Well," Lisa said, "did you set up a profile?"

"Seriously? No! Of course not," I exclaimed.

"Look, Larissa... we're all so proud of you following your dream out in the big city, but we're also worried about you being there all alone. I know it might seem a bit weird, but maybe this is normal for New York. Just set up a profile and see what happens. I've got to go. Love you!"

I thought about what my sister said and decided to do it. The first thing I needed was a picture. I figured out how to use the little camera thing on my phone, and snapped a picture of myself. Still in my work clothes — a baggy, mustard-stained T-shirt and blue jeans with my dark hair tied back in a tight ponytail — it wasn't very sexy. I looked through my clothes and picked out my nicest under things: a matching white bra and panty set. I put them on, and brushed out my hair into a smooth, loose wave. I put on a touch of makeup. Looking in the mirror, I was startled at the effect. I looked sexy.

I sat down and began taking pictures of my newly improved self. After I snapped a shot, I took a look. Gradually, I began taking sexier and more provocative shots — and I found myself turning myself on. I took a close up of my tits, hoisted up in the delicate white bra, and I found my hand wandering into the crisp white panties, feeling the wetness that was developing. I took more pictures. I took a picture of my hand in my panties. I reached behind me and snapped a picture of my round ass. When I was done, I scrolled through my new collection of images, and rubbed my clit. I was surprised and a little embarrassed by how much I'd turned myself on, but couldn't help it. While flicking my clit hard with one had, I stuck a slender finger from the other hand into my pussy. The insertion was too much: I exploded with pleasure, drenching my panties so much that I had to take them off and put them in the laundry basket immediately. I fell asleep where I was, with my phone by my side.

I woke up early the next morning and took a shower. As I scrubbed my body clean, I couldn't stop thinking about how good it felt to cum the night before. I dried off and dressed in my usual baggy uniform then, catching a glimpse of myself in the mirror, decided to change. Instead of a baggy T-shirt, I found the tiniest tank top I could find and pulled it over my head. Much better.

Walking to my stand, I found myself rubbing my hand over the cool plastic of my new phone in my pocket. Without pausing to think, I pulled it out and uploaded some of the sexy shots to a new profile. The thought of people opening the app and seeing me — wet-pussied in my delicate white bra and panties — excited me.

The day at work went incredibly well. Sales were through the roof (I suspect the image of my heaving tits busting out of my cute pink tank top while I prepared my special wieners might have had something to do with it), and my phone was constantly beeping with sexy messages of interest from my Single & Mingle app.

During the mid-afternoon lull, I sat down behind my stand to take a closer look at what people had to say.

"Hot bod! Want to meet up?"

"Man, I would fuck you in those little white panties until they dissolved from you being too wet!"

"Fuck, suck my dick now, sexy!"

While the messages were a tad crass, I couldn't help feeling flattered and turned on. I decided to take a bold new picture to add to my profile. I stood up and looked around: the street was dead at this time of day. I grabbed one of my hot dogs and took a picture of myself taking a deep-throated bite and uploaded it.

Almost immediately, I heard a chime indicating a new response to my S&M app.

It read: "I see you like the app after all... I knew you would. Show me what else you want to do with that wiener."

I froze. It had to be Kyle! At first, I was a bit taken aback: part of what had made things sexy for me at first was the anonymity of it all. Then, I thought about Kyle and his sexy build. Maybe I wouldn't have to cum alone.

Hiding behind my stand, I took another wiener and placed it so that the tip was pressing at the crotch of my pants. I took the picture and uploaded it.

Seconds later, I heard another chime. It was a private message, with an address and the word "tonight."

I arrived at the address at about 8 o'clock that evening. I didn't have any other sexy clothes, so I had to go shopping first — luckily stores in New

York are open late (back home, everything closed at 5 p.m.). I found a super-sexy red lace corset and matching panties and garter, which I put on under my hot dog girl clothes. My plan was to make Kyle work for it, then surprise him with my sexy gear.

The address was an older walk up apartment. Kyle buzzed me, and I walked to the second floor and knocked on his door. Kyle opened it with a huge grin: "I knew I'd see you... in the flesh again," he said.

"I have to admit," I said. "I like the app. But before we do anything, I want to get some pictures of you; your profile was sort of lacking."

"Oh yeah? What kind of pictures?"

I smiled. "Well, first of all, take off your shirt." Kyle obliged, revealing a muscular, though slightly pale chest. "Don't get outside much working at the electronics store?" I joked, and snapped a picture.

"You're getting pretty good with that camera," he said.

"Yeah, I'm a natural," I said. "Now, take off your pants." Kyle unbuttoned and unzipped his jeans, slipping them to his ankles and revealing a bulging package under his boxers. I took a picture.

"Your turn," Kyle said. "Take it off." He

stepped in front of me so that his cock was digging into my clit through our clothes. I stripped to reveal my sexy corset and panties. His cock grew. I took a picture.

Kyle grabbed the phone from my hands. He lifted me so that I was sitting on his kitchen counter and yanked off my panties. He spread my legs and took a picture of my pussy. Then, whipping off his boxers, Kyle slipped his hard dick inside me. He pumped his cock deep inside me — and the shock of his dick suddenly stretching my insides felt amazing.

I grabbed my phone, and took a picture of Kyle's long, thick cock thrusting in and out of me. Then I leaned back and looked at the pictures as he continued to fuck me, enjoying watching our play on the screen while my pussy simultaneously felt the details.

Kyle started fucking me faster. "Fuck, baby, I'm going to come," he cried. I pushed him off of me and jumped off the counter. I knelt in front of him and opened my mouth wide, giving Kyle a target for his cum. He took the hint and, after stroking himself violently for a moment, he came in and around my mouth. I swallowed as much as I could, and then stood up beside him.

"Smile," I said, putting an arm around

him, "That was great." I snapped a picture of Kyle and I standing side-by-side, red-faced and exhausted—with drops of Kyle's thick cum decorating my face and hair.

"Now that's a photo finish," he said. "Let's try for another."

I put my phone in my bag. "Sure... but this time, let's try it the old-fashioned way."

15 SUDS

When I was a little girl, I always knew that I wanted only one thing out of life. I wanted to be a star. I did everything right. I took dance class, singing class, modeling class, and acting class. Since I was 10 years old, I spent every spare moment auditioning, working my craft, or perfecting my body.

By the time I was 22, boy, my body was picture perfect! My body was so toned I could have been a mannequin. My skin was smooth and bronzed. My long, thick hair was tinted to a sweet honey blonde. I had everything. My only problem was, I couldn't seem to land a role if my life depended on it. Then, I found my calling, Soap Operas.

The day I got the callback, for the hot, new Soap Opera "Thorny Avenue," I was over the moon. I loved everything about the show: the makeup; the cameras; the money. It was all super glam.

The only problem was, it was hard to get screen time. My character, Emily, was cast as the "friend" to the show's star, Alexis Facia. So, even when I was on screen, no one was really looking at me. It was always about Alexis. No matter how hard I tried to act, or frankly, how smoking hot I looked, every night, when I checked the show's online message boards, no one ever mentioned me.

I was so close to living my dream, but still not there. I needed to find a way to be the star. So, I decided to take matters into my own hands and make myself a star.

First, I spoke with the producer, Max. We were shooting a party scene that day, so I was fully attired in a glittering gold, sequined gown. My hair was curled and my neck was draped in faux jewels. I knocked on Max's office door. There was no answer, so I let myself in.

Max was at his desk, his head buried

in paperwork. "What do you want," he said, without looking up.

"Hi Max," I said, "I wanted to talk to you a bit, about my character's arc?"

"What?" Max looked up, at me, his eyes tired and his forehead wrinkled with stress. "Look, honey, that's not really something I can help you with. You better get to set."

I smiled at him. "You look exhausted. So stressed," I said. "Let me help you out." I stood behind Max and rubbed his back and shoulders. Max groaned in pleasure. He, obviously, hadn't been touched in a while. I continued leaning over him, so my breasts pressed into the back of his neck, while I massaged his chest from behind.

When I could feel him start to relax, I spun his swivel chair around. Hiking up the skirt of my gown. I straddled Max and ground my crotch into his. Max looked into my eyes for a moment, then, buried his face into my chest.

"Mmm, fuck," he said. He pulled down the straps of my dress and released my tits. He licked and bit at my nipples. I could feel his cock getting harder, in the chair.

"So," I said, grinding my hips down, into his dick. "What do you think? Can we talk some more about my character's arc?"

Max paused for a moment. "Well, you do have a certain 'it' factor. Maybe, we could find your character a love interest? I think you might have a knack for it. Maybe, you could show me what you've got?"

I grinned. "Absolutely." I turned around and motioned for Max to unzip my dress. Once it slid off, I was totally naked. I knelt down, in front of Max's chair, and unzipped his pants, releasing a raging boner. Looking up, at him, I licked the tip of his cock. Teasingly, I licked his dick in sections: under the shaft; on its sides; under the crest of the tip. Then, I used my whole mouth to suck in his cock. Coming up for air, I spit on Max's dick, and started massaging his slippery cock with my hand. He leaned back and groaned.

"How's that? Worthy of a love scene?" I asked.

"I'm not sure yet," Max said. "What else have you got?"

I leaned over Max's desk, placing my elbows on his stack of paperwork and sticking my round ass in his face. Max groped my ass cheeks, and slapped them. He stood up and slid his dick, still dripping wet from my saliva, into my equally damp pussy. I bucked back against him, pushing my hips hard into his.

"Fuck, your pussy is so wet!" Max screamed.

"Yeah? I bet this ass would look good on screen," I said.

"Mmm. Fuck yes. Let me see some other angles, though," he said. He pulled out of me and flipped me over. I sat on his desk, as the paperwork went flying to the ground. He pushed me back and pulled my hips to the edge of the desk. Max shoved his cock inside me and started pumping, furiously. I held on to the edge of the desk, as it thumped against the ground. Finally, Max screamed, cumming hard inside my pussy. With one final pump, he pulled out, dragging a stream of white cum out, after him.

He pulled his pants back on, and I stepped into my dress. He zipped me up.

"So?" I asked.

"Yeah, yeah. You've got it. I'll talk to the writers about expanding your role," he said. I grinned; rushing off to set with the feeling of Max's warm cum still streaming down my leg.

Max did not disappoint. A week later, a new storyline was introduced, where my character started a flirtation with her boss, played by a handsome, dark-haired fox named Daniel.

In the show, Daniel was Alexis's on and off boyfriend. So, having my character mess with him was a huge deal, one I was sure, was the producer Max's doing. I was thrilled.

I trolled the show's message boards online. My character was finally getting the attention she deserved, sparking a lot of controversy.

"Emily's really starting to grow on me!" One commentator said.

"She has a certain appeal, but is she as sexy as Alexis?" Another said.

Concerned that my star might wane, I decided to be sure I made an impression. It was time to step things up on screen. So, when my character had her first on-screen love scene with Daniel, I decided to do whatever it took to show the viewers how steamy I could be.

The love scene took place in a bubble bath. Because Soaps want to make things look realistic, but can't show any actual nudity, they often depend on this kind of set piece. I was given a flesh-toned swimsuit, to wear in the tub, but I had other ideas.

In the scene, Emily is taking a sensual

bath, when Daniel accidently walks in, and they have a sexy bath together. I was going to play the scene by the book, but... sexier.

I climbed into the tub on set and, below the bubbles, slipped out of the swimsuit. Sitting naked in the tub, surrounded by the crew and cameras, I felt my pussy getting excited in anticipation.

Daniel walked on set and the director called, "Action."

"Emily," Daniel said, in character, "I couldn't stay away. I've been thinking about you all day."

"Oh, Daniel," I said, "I've been thinking about you, too. I can't resist you!"

Daniel knelt by the tub, and leaned in. "But, we can't be together..." He started to speak, but froze. His eyes widening, as he felt my nakedness beneath the bubbles.

"Cut!" The director yelled. "Forget your line? Come on man, we've got to shoot the whole love scene before lunch."

I winked at Daniel. "Yeah," I said. "Let's do this."

The director called, "Action," and we started, again.

"Emily," Daniel said, "I couldn't stay away. I've been thinking about you all day."

"Oh, Daniel," I said, "I've been thinking about you, too. I can't resist you!"

Daniel knelt by the tub, and leaned in. "But, we can't be together... I don't know what to do."

"Then," I said, seductively, "Just do me."

We kissed, passionately.

"Maybe, we should have something to drink," Daniel said. He poured "champagne" (sparkling apple juice) from the bottle beside the tub, into flutes, and gave me one. I took a sip and set it down.

Daniel took off his white robe and slid into the tub, beside me. "Emily, I think I love you," he said. We kissed in the slow, visual way you do on camera, but under the water I grabbed Daniel's cock from his flesh-colored swim trunks and found that he was already hard.

"This is wrong. What if Alexis finds out," he said, as he slid his fingers into my pussy with one hand, while propping himself up, over top of me. I couldn't help but moan softly.

"She'll never know," I said, kissing him, again, and slipping his cock into my pussy with my hand. Our faces were inches apart. I could feel his cock stretching my pussy, but we didn't dare move lest anyone know what we were doing.

"Cut!" The director called. "Guys, that was amazing! I've never seen a scene that hot. Great work. Ok! Moving on!"

We slipped back into our suits and got out of the tub, as the crew moved on, to another scene with other actors.

I practically skipped to my dressing room, thrilled with how successful the scene had been, and titillated by me and Daniel's mini-fuck.

I walked into the room, and slipped into a blue silk robe. I lay down on my couch and thought about how wonderful the scene would play on camera. Thinking about our bathtub adventure, I felt my pussy getting wetter and wetter. I reached down and touched my clit. I closed my eyes and started rubbing harder and faster. I was getting close, when, suddenly, I felt warm breath on my pussy. I opened my eyes.

The actor that played Daniel was kneeling beside the couch, his mouth tantalizingly close to my crotch.

"I was thinking that, maybe, we could... rehearse," he said. "We should really perfect our scenes, so that it comes across realistic."

"I couldn't agree more," I said. "Start right where you are."

Dutifully, he licked my pussy, focusing his tongue on the crest of my clit. I grabbed his hair and pushed his head further into me. He reached up and grabbed my tits, squeezing them so hard that it almost hurt. I let him eat me, until I was just about to cum. Then, I pulled him up to me, by the hair.

"Show me how you'd fuck me," I said. He kissed me, then, grabbed my right ankle and pushed it up, behind my head. He, then, shoved his hard cock into my slit. Using my leg as a handle, he pounded me hard, on the couch. Then, he grabbed my other leg and pushed it behind my head, so that I was practically folded in half. He fucked me hard.

"Show me how you'd cum on me," I said. He thrust into me, one last time, then, pulled out and grabbed his dick. He pumped himself with his hand for a moment, then, came hard, on my tits, squirting tendrils of semen all over me.

He grabbed a tissue from the table beside the couch and wiped me clean. Then, he lay on top of me.

"You know," he said. "I think we might be on to something here. I've seen you and your hot body in the shadows. You're not the only one who wants more screen time. Maybe, if we start showing the stay-at-home moms, who watch our show, some real, steamy scenes, they'll start showing us more," he said.

I smiled. "You've got yourself a deal."

16 FIERCE COMPETITION

I'll tell you one thing: I never had a problem getting noticed before I entered the Miss. Tropics pageant, and I didn't like it.

I don't want to sound cocky, but I was always used to being the hottest girl in the room. It's not my fault—I was born this way. Basically, I'm a hotter and more human version of Barbie, with my waist-length, glossy blonde hair, perfect tits, tiny waist, and cantaloupe ass.

So, for as long as I could remember, I'd made my money with my looks. Modeling, being a trophy girlfriend and winning beauty pageants allowed me to live the high life. But then, I entered that damn pageant and everything changed.

The first round of competition was

just walking around on the stage with all 50 of us contestants wearing matching skintight black cat suits for the judges. Backstage, I was scorching. Looking at myself if the mirror, I was totally tight and my ass was popping perfectly. I would have fucked myself right there if I could have, but before long, we were told to line up to go on stage.

"And, from Orange Country, please welcome Victoria Cox!" The MC announced, and I strutted on stage with a flip of my hair. I blew a kiss at the judges table like I always did, but was horrified to see that none of them were even looking up. I stood on my mark and swiveled my hips a bit to show off my best angle. Still nothing. I squeezed my shoulders together so that my tits looked huge. Not a look.

"And now, from San Diego, please welcome Malia Scott!" The MC announced the next girl, so I walked off the little duct tape X on the floor to the other side of the stage and watched. When Malia went to center stage, everyone's head turned. Malia was the opposite of me: she's tiny, shorter than most pageant girls at maybe 5 foot 3, and she had dark, bobbed hair. Her body was almost androgynous, lithe. I couldn't believe it. There was even some spattered applause as she posed.

"Unbelievable," I seethed.

After the intro walk, there was a half-hour break for the girls to change for the swimwear round and for the stage hands to switch the sets to a glimmering beach scene. Being a pro, I was in my red python print string bikini in minutes and ready to go. As I preened in the mirror, I saw the Malia girl surrounded by admirers.

"Oh Malia, you're so going to win. What are you going to do with the cash?" A ditzy girl cooed to Malia. Hearing that was enough for me: I wasn't going to let some ugly girl take my crown.

I left the backstage area and looked down the hall for the judges' dressing room and knocked on the door.

"Come in," a deep male voice called out. I walked in slowly.

The two male judges were lounging on a plush couch in the middle of the room. I plopped myself between them and arched my back. Without looking up from his phone, one of the judges said: "Look, you can't be in here. Get out and back to the stage area before we call Alice and get you kicked out."

I couldn't believe it. No man had ever talked to me like that before. I took it in stride.

"Oh, I just wanted to introduce myself to you boys... I noticed it was a bit hard to get your attention earlier," I said.

The second judge, a slightly pudgy man with piercing blue eyes, looked up from his phone and sighed. "Look, sweetie, we're really busy here."

Figuring that blue eyes were more approachable, I turned my attention to him. I placed my hand on his thigh and started stroking gentle circles over his suit pants. He shifted his weight on the couch. Bingo.

"I was just worried that I didn't have your attention before, so I want to show you some of what I can do now," she said. I unzipped his pants and pulled out his cock, which was already half hardened at my touch. I leaned over and licked the tip delicately, looking up at him with my huge, false eyelashed eyes. The judge's dick was instantly rock hard. I spat on it and then alternated between stroking it fast with my tiny, manicured hand and sucking the tip with my glossy lips.

"Fuck," he moaned, leaning back on the couch, he reached to my back and pulled the string on the back of my bikini—my tits popped out and into his lap. The judge squeezed them aggressively. "Is this what you want, you slut?" I nodded and smiled, sucking harder and cupping his balls.

Suddenly, I felt hands on my ass. "For

fuck's sake, how am I supposed to ignore this?" The other judge said from behind me. "Gloria's going to kill me." I felt the second judge's finger probing at my pussy from behind through my bikini bottom.

There was a knock at the door. "Gary? Mark? You're on in two."

The pudgy judge, apparently Gary, cleared his throat. "Be right there," he yelled to the door. He turned to me, "this isn't over." I smiled, re-tied my top and pranced to the door. I turned and blew the judges a kiss as they hastily adjusted their hard cocks in their pants.

The swimsuit round went much better than the others. While the female judge gave me a bitchy, condescending smirk while I was on stage, Gary and Mark seemed much more interested in what my body had to say.

After the swimsuit round, I rushed back to adjust my flowing blonde curls and slipped into my glittering backless evening gown before rushing back to the dressing room. I knocked on the door and entered before I could hear a response.

Inside, I was horrified to see a tiny

dark bob bobbing up and down on judge Mark's erect cock.

"What the fuck!" I yelled.

Malia turned her head. "What, you thought you were the only one who could suck a cock?"

I lunged at the bitch. "Fuck you!" Judge Gary pulled me off of Malia, who was topless with a shimmering navy gown at her waist.

Gary's cock was out of his pants. "Maybe we could have a bit of a competition in here... ladies?"

I glared at Malia. I wasn't going to let this skinny bitch win. I pulled my long skirt up to my waist and straddled Gary. I reached down to my pussy and found it was surprisingly wet already: apparently, the excitement of competition really turned me on. I eased my pussy onto the tip of Gary's hard dick, teasing him just a bit, letting him feel my juices drip down his shaft. Soon, he couldn't take it any longer and pushed me down, impaling me with his cock. I screamed. Gary grabbed my ass cheeks and used them as handles to bounce me up and down frantically on his cock. "Oh, fuck yeah, Victoria!" he screamed.

On the couch beside us, I saw that Malia noticed that I had upped my game, but she kept just sucking Mark's cock. "Why can't you fuck me like that? Fuck me now." Mark said, obviously feeling jealous that his friend was enjoying my juicy pussy. Malia tentatively stepped out of her dress and straddled Mark. I couldn't help but notice that her body, while thin, was pretty sexy.

Side by side, Malia and I rode the judges — both of us trying harder and harder to make our respective judges come. Mark and Gary seemed to be in heaven, and after a while, I noticed Malia staring at my heaving tits as they bounced wildly. I grabbed her hand and put it on my boob. She bit her lip, then leaned over and kissed me while still fucking the judge.

"Holy shit," Gary said. Watching two beautiful women kiss must have been too much for him, as he exploded with cum inside of me, blasting load after load deep into my pussy. He slapped my ass. "Bonus point, gorgeous."

I climbed off of Gary and sat on the couch beside him, catching my breath as cum dripped out of my already wet pussy. Mark looked over at me. "Fuck that's hot. Malia, don't you want to taste that."

Malia seemed eager to oblige. She climbed off of Mark's hard rod and knelt in front of me. She lapped the cum and pussy juice from my crotch. Mark got off of the couch and stood behind her, shoving his dick inside of Malia as she licked my pussy. I could feel every thrust that he pushed into her, as it shoved her tongue deeper and deeper inside me.

Then again, there was a knock on the door. "Two minutes, guys!" The judges' assistant called out from the hallway.

"I'm coming!" Gary called out.

"Fuck," Mark said, his cock still throbbing as Malia and I rushed to get back in our gowns and out to the final category in the pageant.

Out on stage, I was still incredibly turned on. I could feel drops of cum streaming slowly down my leg, and my pussy throbbed from beneath my gown. Still, I was professional. I strutted my sexy ass around the stage, and stepped up to the microphone.

The female judge asked me my question: "Victoria, what do you think is the most important factor in a woman's happiness in today's world?"

"Well," I said with my biggest, whitest pageant smile. "I believe that keeping on top of your game and staying sexually satisfied is the best way to truly be happy." A hush fell over the stunned crowd. No one had ever given such an honest answer, but I knew what I was doing. Looking at Gary and Mark, it was clear who was going to get the most points and the crown that night.

Stepping back into line on the stage, I waited while the other girls said their piece and daydreamed about my new crown and $5,000 cash prize. Then, I felt a hand caress my pussy over the front of my dress. Malia stood in front of me on the stage, and had reached her hand behind her to stroke my pussy. I reached forward and rubbed my hand over Malia's tiny, tight ass. We stroked each other so feverishly that the other girls in line started to notice and edged away from us, but we didn't care. I felt my pussy getting hotter and wetter as she rubbed at my clit through my dress until finally I climaxed so hard that I had to lean forward on Malia's back.

I was walking on air, still cumming a bit by the time it came to announcing the winners. We started as a big group, and gradually the other girl's were eliminated one by one until it was just Malia and me left on stage. We held hands, as you always do in pageants, but with special significance as we could still smell each other's sex on our palms. She squeezed me tight.

"And the first runner up is..." The female judge said, building suspense.

"Victoria Cox! Which means that our winner tonight, taking home the crown and the $5,000 cash prize, is Malia Scott!"

I was shocked. I dropped her hand abruptly. I never, ever lost. I watched as Malia accepted the crown, my crown, and the money with a grin from Gary. She turned back towards me and smiled mischievously.

Backstage, I stood and waited until Malia's admirers had had their chance to speak with her.

"Nice job," I said, forcing a congenial smile.

"No, really, I couldn't have done it without you." Malia said. "Shall we celebrate?"

"What did you have in mind?" I asked suspiciously.

"Well," she said, "I don't know about you... but I'm not finished with those judges yet."

"I don't know. I'm kind of mad at those guys still... no offense," I said, playing with my long hair as it streamed over my shoulder.

"Oh, fuck those Mark and Gary guys," Malia said, guiding me down the hall and opening a door. Inside, the female judge lounged on a couch wearing nothing but a pale pink laced corset and thigh high stockings. She smiled up at us   while   she   stroked   herself.

"Well, if it isn't my queens," the judge said. I smiled at Malia, and shut the door behind us.

The End

AUTHOR'S NOTE

Readers: I want to expand a few of the stories to see where the characters can be explored further. If there are any of the stories that you would like to read more about again, I'd love to hear from you!

Visit my blog at www.melisapoche.com

Join my newsletter for free exclusive previews
www.melisapoche.com/in

Follow me on Twitter at
www.twitter.com/melisapoche

Like my page on Facebook at
http://www.facebook.com/melisapoche2

Discover my books at major ebook retailers everywhere.